the WARRIOR in the mist

OTHER TITLES FROM RUTH EASTHAM

The Memory Cage

The Messenger Bird

Arrowhead

The Jaguar Trials

Ruth Eastham

the WARRIOR in the mist

www.shrinebell.com

to

Caroline Johnson

Warrior Queen

First published in 2017 by Shrine Bell, an imprint of Vertebrate Publishing.

Shrine Bell
Crescent House, 228 Psalter Lane, Sheffield, S11 8UT, UK.
www.shrinebell.com

Cover design by Nathan Ryder at Ryder Design – www.ryderdesign.studio
Typesetting and production by Jane Beagley.
Author photograph © Ruth Eastham.

A CIP catalogue record for this book is available from the British Library.

ISBN 978-1-911342-38-0 (Paperback)
ISBN 978-1-911342-39-7 (Ebook)

10 9 8 7 6 5 4 3 2 1

Production by Vertebrate Publishing
www.v-publishing.co.uk

Shrine Bell and Vertebrate Publishing are committed to printing on paper from sustainable sources.

Printed and bound in Great Britain by Clays Ltd, St Ives plc.

EVERY YEAR CARRUS VILLAGE REMEMBERS ...
WHEN BRITAIN WAS UNDER ROMAN RULE.
WHEN THE WARRIOR QUEEN BOUDICCA
AND HER TRIBE FOUGHT BACK.
CARRUS REMEMBERS ...
AD61
THE LAST, GREAT, TERRIBLE BATTLE.
CHARIOT WARFARE, SPEAR,
BOW AND ARROW, SWORD.

NOBODY KNEW WHERE THAT BATTLE
TOOK PLACE TWO THOUSAND YEARS AGO.
NOBODY KNEW WHAT HAPPENED
TO BOUDICCA AND HER DAUGHTERS.
NOBODY KNEW THE TRUTH.

UNTIL NOW.

Engraving at the entrance to the
Carrus World Heritage Museum.

Part 1

1

BLUE FIRE

'Come on, Centurion!' Aidan tugged at the rope, leading the horse across the meadow. 'You need to get to your paddock!'

Aidan looked towards Carrus Woods, at the drilling tower beyond the trees. He felt the morning sun on his face. He should have been at the big anti-fracking demonstration ages ago. His mates Emmi and Jon would already be there, Dad too.

Fracking. Aidan remembered what he'd felt when he'd first read about it. Drilling long shafts deep underground. Blasting water into the shale rock to get the gas out.

He pulled the halter, harder than he'd meant to, and Centurion let out a rumbling snort.

'Sorry, boy.' Aidan gave him a hurried pat. 'Easy.'

Horses whinnied loudly to them from the fence at the far side of the wide meadow. Firefly and Fenland Queen, two of the other horses on the Berryman estate where

Aidan's dad worked.

He felt a pang in his chest. Mum was gone, and soon the horses would be too.

Aidan's eyes travelled over the brownish grass of the meadow. Light sparked off the water of its shrunken lake. A couple of magpies pecked the drought-cracked ground between gorse bushes. A hare ran across the space.

His mobile phone blared out from his pocket.

EMMI CALLING.

'Where *are* you, Aidan?' There were loud noises in the background, as if she was in the middle of a battlefield or something. 'You need to get here fast. The trucks will be arriving any minute!'

'You're missing the action, Aide!' Jon must have grabbed the phone off her. 'It's all turning nasty!' he said enthusiastically. 'Some important guy from Enershale is trying to talk to the crowds, but they keep shouting him down. And the press have just rolled up. You're gonna lose your chance to be on the telly!'

Enershale. That was the big company with plans to do the fracking; what the protest was all about.

And the reason Dad was about to lose his job looking after the horses.

'Just got to get Centurion in his paddock,' Aidan told him.

'He knocked over his food bucket and I had to spend ages ... '

Aidan's low-battery warning gave a beep.

'We need you!' Emmi was back on the line. 'We've got your protest placard here ready and ... ' A harsh honking drowned out her voice, one of those hooter things. The same sound, fainter, came at Aidan from across the woods. He thought about the slogan on his placard as he clicked off his phone:

DON'T TAKE OUR LAND!

'Let's go, Centurion!' It was going to take forever to get all the way across the meadow at this rate. Centurion stamped a front hoof on the ground, looking across at the other horses, impatient to be with them.

Aidan fidgeted with the rope.

There *was* a faster way.

His heart beat hard. The last time Dad caught him riding Centurion, he'd not been happy. Given him a massive lecture about the horse being too big and headstrong and powerful for him. He'd been so overprotective and stuff since Mum ... Aidan swallowed. Since Mum died.

And his dad's boss, the landowner, Lord James Berryman, wouldn't take kindly to anyone breaking the rules about riding.

Aidan pulled at his bottom lip. But what did he care about following Berryman's rules? He was kicking Aidan and his dad off the estate as soon as the fracking started.

My business interests with Enershale have to be my focus from now on. Lord Berryman's voice spooled through Aidan's head. *And the horse paddocks will be needed for the next phase of operations.*

Aidan tried to push away his worries about leaving. He reached up to stroke the horse's silky nose and felt a rush of hot breath on his fingers. He could control Centurion. He had before, plenty of times, when Dad was off working round the estate. There was no saddle, only the halter, and rope looped into makeshift reins; but still.

He slowly rubbed Centurion's mahogany neck, talking quietly. The horse's nostrils flared; his huge dark brown eyes glittered.

Aidan gripped a handful of black mane and vaulted on to his back. He pressed the horse's flanks lightly with his heels and the animal gave an approving snort and immediately broke into a trot.

The hooter sounded again. Faint shouts could be heard from across the woodland. The waiting horses neighed. Centurion's ears were laid back flat against his head and Aidan felt the pace increase a touch. He smiled at the feeling of movement rippling under him. Centurion might be past his prime, but he was far from past it!

Seconds passed. Shapes darted overhead; some kind of hawk, hunting down a smaller bird. The other horses were ahead of them, pressed together and skittish.

'Steady!' They were cantering now. Aidan leant back on the rope to ease Centurion up a bit, but the horse gave a stubborn toss of the head.

Faster.

The sun was hot on the back of Aidan's neck as he crouched forward, gripping tight with his knees. He glanced at the other horses, side by side watching.

Galloping now.

Aidan pulled on the rope, trying to regain control. There was the noise of a helicopter approaching – a news team, maybe, heading for the protest – and Centurion's body tensed. Aidan wrapped the cord around his fist. He pulled harder, the fibres digging into his hands, burning them.

The chopper skimmed overhead; the whirling blades blasting through the air, and Centurion shuddered with a wild energy. The horse put on a surge of speed.

'Stop!' Aidan's heart pounded. Clumps of dry grass were torn up from the ground. The magpies rose into the air, cawing raucously.

The muscles along the horse's neck quivered. Their merged shadows stretched ahead of them as Centurion raced forward. 'Stop!'

They approached the lake in the middle of the meadow, hooves slamming against the ground. A line of cloud moved over the sun. Aidan heard Centurion's sharp breaths; manic whinnying from the horses up ahead.

And then, in mid-gallop, without warning, fire flared up from the surface of the lake.

Fire?

What the ... ?

Two pale blue flames.

Centurion reared with a cry. The rope was wrenched from Aidan's hands. He clung to the mane as the animal stumbled and swayed.

'*Centurion!*' Aidan lost his grip and was thrown. He slammed on to a gorse bush and rolled, one arm twisting; blurred twigs and thorns scratched his skin. He heard the thud of Centurion hitting the ground; a high-pitched neigh.

Aidan lay face down, chest heaving. The dry grass spiked his face, and he smelt the earthy tang of baked soil. He dragged himself up into a sitting position, then stumbled over to where Centurion was lying and knelt by his head.

The horse's dark eyes were wide, his mouth gnashing hard.

'*Centurion.*'

Aidan was vaguely aware of a pain in his arm; the other horses' alarmed neighs. He saw a front leg, bent awkwardly; a smear of blood.

Centurion was trying to get up.

'Keep still.' Aidan stroked the horse's clammy neck. 'Don't move.' He felt a queasy panic as he thought about what a bad leg injury could mean. If a bone was broken. If the owner, Berryman, found out ... *What if he had Centurion put down; like Velvet Dancer had been that time?*

Aidan stared at the lake. *Fire on water?* How could that have happened? He scrutinised the surface, but saw nothing more than grey-green wind ripples.

Aidan fumbled to pull his phone from his jeans pocket. His hands were shaking so much it was hard to swipe the screen. It seemed to ring for an age before it was answered.

'Dad! It's Centurion!' The words came out in a garbled rush. 'He's hurt!'

'Didn't catch that, son.' Dad sounded distant and there was shouting in the background. 'Where ... you?' His voice was breaking up and there was a splutter of static. 'Say ... again.'

'You have to come!'

'What? ... say – '

The battery cut out.

Aidan turned back to Centurion, smoothing tangles from his mane. For a moment he was torn between going for help and staying to look after the horse.

'It'll be OK,' he whispered. 'It'll all be ... ' His voice trailed off.

Those were the same words.

The exact same words Dad had told him, when Mum had first got ill.

And then he was on his feet and running – across the meadow. Sprinting over the parched grass towards Carrus Woods.

2

INVASION

Aidan ran, heading in the direction of the protest. The sun was in his eyes; his trainers pounding the dry grass. He held his throbbing arm against his chest, clutching his wrist with the other hand.

All he could think about was Centurion, lying in the meadow.

Centurion ... Mum's favourite ...

A dull headache started over one eye. *My fault. My fault ...* The hooter sounded from somewhere ahead. Faint shouts carried towards him.

Aidan plunged into the woods and raced along the shady path that wound between the trunks.

Need to find Dad. Get help.

Sticks snapped under his feet. Bushes snagged his clothes. Foliage closed in to block the light. The hooter sounded again, louder and more urgently, like an alarm siren.

Aidan came into a clearing. He skidded to a stop by the

mound that rose from its centre. An ancient-looking horse chestnut tree grew on its top, its thick roots like fingers clutching the surface of the little hill. Wisps of blueish mist lingered in the shadows.

There was someone there.

A figure half hidden by the tree's dense, twisting branches.

'Do you have a phone?' he called. 'It's my horse!'

Sweat stung Aidan's eyes. It was hard to make out the figure in the gloomy haze. A woman? Strangely dressed, in a cloak or something. Probably in some kind of fancy dress, on her way to the protest. But she didn't move; didn't react. She didn't seem even to have heard him.

'He's hurt!' Aidan started to climb towards her, a crust of soil coming away as he scrambled up. The clearing was completely still, a weird pocket of silence. No birdsong, nothing.

'Do you have a mobile I can borrow, please?' he said, more uncertainly.

He blinked hard, rubbing his eyes, peering into the shadows, but he could no longer see the woman.

Only the huge, half-dead tree with its gnarled bark and twisted branches.

Aidan stared in confusion, then slid down the mound and dashed on along the trail.

The shouts from beyond the woodland got louder. A drum beat. Whistles. Aidan's legs ached, but he sprinted hard along the snaking path. A voice blared through a megaphone: *'ARE WE REALLY GOING TO STAND BY WHILE THE FRACKERS RUIN OUR LAND? THESE ARE THE ANCIENT CARRUS WOODS AND THE LAND SHOULD BE LEFT ALONE!'*

Aidan turned a corner and found himself out of the trees and in a crowd.

RESTRICTED AREA. A flag with the Enershale eagle emblem fluttered from the top of a steel mesh, making the bird look like it was swooping on to some unseen prey. He was being jostled from every side. 'Please! Can I get past?' he cried over the deafening noise.

Placards swung about over his head. *GRASSLAND, NOT GAS LAND ... NOT FOR SHALE*. Hands were raised in fists as people chanted. Aidan saw a group of police officers in fluorescent vests keeping a watchful distance. He tripped on the guy rope of a protestor's tent.

Aidan looked wildly around in the din, scanning the faces. He saw Miss Carter, the drama teacher from his school; he saw Emmi's tall older cousin, Robbie, with his spiked white-blond hair and patchwork waistcoat.

And finally there was Dad, at the far side of the crowd,

wearing his first aider's vest. Aidan tried to push his way through to him, but the mass of people pressed him back.

Protestors were stringing a banner across the gate to the sound of fierce clapping: *NO ENTRY. FRACK-FREE ZONE.* Aidan glanced at the drilling tower and the tall chimney stack beyond; the water tanks and the mounds of sand.

The crowd parted a moment, but before Aidan could push forward, Emmi and Jon appeared in the gap, shoving a placard into his hand: *DON'T TAKE OUR LAND!*

'The trucks taking supplies to the drilling platform will be arriving any minute!' Emmi yelled.

Aidan caught hold of her, shouting to make himself heard. '*Centurion's hurt!*'

Jon frowned. '*What?*'

Aidan let his placard fall to the ground. All he cared about at that moment was Centurion. He peered desperately through the crowd, but he'd lost sight of Dad.

'Centurion fell! I need your phone, Emmi – NOW!'

She started to fish out her mobile. The crowd surged forward, jamming the three of them together, and jostling them towards the compound gate.

There was the growl of engines. Tension like a ripple of heat. Faces turned to look down the long gravel road. People linked elbows to block the gate.

Aidan saw Miss Carter raise a loudhailer to her mouth. 'OUR RICH HISTORY IS UNDER THREAT!' Loud cheers. 'A HISTORY STRETCHING BACK THOUSANDS OF YEARS THROUGH THE MISTS OF TIME! TO THE ERA OF ROMAN INVASION.' A dust haze appeared at the far end of the road and a lorry came into view.

'TO THE ERA WHEN QUEEN BOUDICCA LED HER ICENI TRIBE INTO BATTLE IN DEFENCE OF THEIR LAND!' There was the grinding rattle of gears, and the wall of people across the entrance shuffled closer together.

Aidan had a fleeting sensation of being part of something; he couldn't place it – not here, not now, but in some other time.

'NOW THERE IS A NEW THREAT TO OUR LAND – A NEW BATTLE.'

Dad!

Aidan glimpsed him again and forced his way through the mass of people.

'AND JUST AS OUR ANCIENT CELTIC ANCESTORS FOUGHT BACK ALL THOSE CENTURIES AGO – SO SHALL WE!'

'Dad!' Aidan blurted as he reached him.

'Centurion fell. I was riding him ... His leg ... '

'What?' Dad gripped him by the shoulders. 'Are you hurt?'

Aidan shook his head.

The truck rumbled closer to the blockade. There was the glare of sunlight off its steel cab.

Along the edges of the road, protestors held placards – red paint running so it looked like blood. *STOP THE FRACKING.* The relentless drumbeat pounded in time. '*STOP! STOP! STOP!*'

'Need to get out of this damn mess!' shouted Dad. 'Get the vet.' But the crowd had closed in tight around them again. Aidan tried to push his way through. The lorry was so close now that he could smell the diesel fumes. There was the shuddering hiss of brakes ...

But then someone in the wall must have lost their nerve. One person was all it took. Aidan saw the protesters sway, a woman fall. The human barrier tilted forward. Broke. He saw the police moving in.

The crowd scattered outwards, and Aidan was able to get free in the chaos. He saw a tent get trampled; a guy rope snapped up like a whip. He saw his cardboard placard on the ground, all bashed up. TAKE ... OUR ... LAND.

And then the four of them were running together – Aidan leading the way, Dad on his phone trying to get through to the vet. Away from the protest, away from the battle; Aidan praying that they weren't too late.

The queen feels her daughters press close. Pounding hooves tear the marshy ground. Clods of sodden earth spin from their chariot's wheels. She slams her whip at the horses, their manes in leaping tangles. The girls stare out, their grey-green eyes wide; one with her cloak edged in fur; the other with auburn hair braided in a great plait. Behind is the woodland; ahead a moving knot of bloodied bodies ...

3

CROSS MY HEART

Aidan sat by Centurion in the hot meadow, unpicking the knots in the horse's mane. He watched the vet run a hand over the animal's swollen leg.

Please don't be broken, Aidan pleaded inwardly. Dad pressed a hand on his shoulder. *Please!*

'What's the diagnosis?' asked Jon, biting his thumbnail.

'He is going to be all right, isn't he?' Emmi asked anxiously.

Ann, the vet, continued to inspect the knee.

Aidan heard whinnying and saw Firefly and Fenland Queen by the fence at the far side of the field.

'What happened out here, Aidan?' his dad asked quietly, so only he could hear. 'After what I told you about not riding him, how could you have disobeyed me like that?' He sounded more hurt than angry.

'It was the flames ... ' Aidan mumbled. 'On the lake.' He wouldn't be surprised if Dad didn't believe him; he hardly believed it himself.

Dad screened his eyes and looked over the lake. 'Maybe sunlight reflected off the water. The glare got him spooked.'

Aidan decided not to argue. 'I'm really sorry,' he said.

Dad gave a short nod. 'I'm just glad you're OK.'

Aidan felt the painful throb in his arm, but what was that compared to what had happened to Centurion? He pressed his hand into his pocket.

'Yeah, I'm fine.'

'Well, the good news is there're no bones broken,' Ann told them.

'Really?' Aidan grinned and he heard Dad let out a relieved sigh.

'That's great!' said Emmi. 'For a minute I was really, really worried! If the leg had been broken and Lord Berryman had found out – '

'Hang on, hang on,' the vet raised a hand to interrupt her.

Aidan stopped smiling.

'Ligaments have been badly strained,' said Ann with a frown. 'Recovery is hard to predict. But with the right treatment and healing time ... '

'I'll pay for any treatment Centurion needs,' Aidan's dad said quickly.

Ann lowered her voice. 'I'll be honest with you, Martin, it's going to cost a fair amount to put it right. He'll need a course of anti-inflammatory injections, and I'll have to do an ultrasound scan in a few days, to get a true understanding of the extent of the injury.'

Aidan glanced at Dad. They both knew money was tight. Dad had spent all he had, and more, on trying to get Mum well.

'Meanwhile, cold therapy will help take down the swelling.' Ann pressed a rubbery ice pack on to the horse's leg. 'Surely Berryman's insurance can cover the treatment costs,' she said. 'I'll need to get his approval with a signature, of course.'

'Oh, Lord Berryman can't find out about the injury!' cried Emmi. 'Even if there are no broken bones, he could still use it as an excuse to have Centurion put down. If the fracking happens he'll get rid of the horses, and he won't be able to sell an injured one.'

'Yeah,' Jon nodded. 'He'll use the horses for the Iceni Festival one last time to impress his girlfriends, and then that's it!'

Aidan's chest went tight. *The festival! The day after tomorrow.* He'd completely forgotten he was supposed to be using Centurion in the chariot race!

Ann filled a syringe with liquid from a small bottle. 'If you ask me, it's no coincidence the fracking's scheduled for the same day as the festival. It's an attempt to distract people's attention.' She stroked Centurion's leg then pushed in the needle. 'That should ease the pain for you, old boy.'

The vet gave a small shake of her head. 'But listen – do you really think Lord Berryman will have Centurion put down? He must know how important he is to you and your dad, Aidan.'

The old Lord Berryman knew, thought Aidan. But things had been different since the young Lord Berryman took over.

Centurion. Aidan swallowed. *Mum had named him when he was a foal.*

Aidan heard Dad's voice catch as he spoke: 'I'll pay for the treatment.'

'Even though you'll have to leave him,' Ann reminded him quietly, 'once the fracking starts?'

Dad stood a little straighter. 'I know it might not be for much longer, Ann,' he said. 'But while the horses are still in my care, I'll do whatever I can for Centurion.'

Aidan felt a flush of pride.

Ann looked at Aidan's dad, then gave a stiff nod.

'And who's to say the fracking *will* ever start, anyway?' said Emmi. 'The protest's not over yet, and we've still got two whole days! People power can still stop it – and you saw the TV cameras!'

'I made sure they got a good close-up of my banner,' added Jon. 'The footage is already on YouTube!'

'And there's the community meeting at the museum this evening,' Emmi went on. 'To weigh up our final options.'

Jon rolled his eyes at Aidan. *'Bo-ring!'* he mouthed.

Aidan caught Ann's arm. 'So you won't tell Lord Berryman about Centurion?'

The vet gave a long, drawn-out sigh, then winked. 'Cross my heart,' she said.

'What this horse needs now is to get out of the sun and have plenty of rest.' She crooked an elbow round the animal's neck, ushering him to his feet. 'Martin, give me a hand, will you?'

Aidan followed as Ann and Dad led the limping horse towards the stables.

'Centurion will be OK, Aide,' said Jon as they went, and Aidan tried to return a smile.

'Hey, why don't we go and get the chariot ready for the race?' suggested Jon. 'Test it out with Firefly or Fenland Queen.'

'Yes, great idea!' Emmi pulled on Aidan's hand. 'Take your mind off ... '

The sound of a car engine interrupted their conversation. A vehicle was making its way towards the estate. Sunlight reflected off the metallic red bodywork. It was a convertible, with the top down, and little needles pricked Aidan's stomach. Only one person round here had a car like that.

'Berryman's coming!' he hollered at Dad. 'Get Centurion out of sight!'

'They won't reach the stables in time!' Emmi said in alarm.

'We've got to delay him!' Aidan leapt through the hedge and sprinted towards the cattle grid, his friends following. He knew Berryman would have to slow down at the grid.

The red Porsche rounded the corner. There was a screech of brakes and the car stopped in a rush of spitting gravel. Berryman's thin, boyish face poked out.

'What do you think you're doing?' his voice whined over the purr of the engine. 'I nearly killed you!'

'Sorry Lord Berryman,' panted Aidan, thinking fast. He glanced past the man's shoulder. He could see Dad and Ann with Centurion, close to the stables, but still in full view.

'There's a big pothole up ahead that we needed to warn you about. Dad hasn't had time to repair it yet.'

'Pothole?' Berryman ran his fingers through his long blonde hair. 'I'm perfectly capable of driving round it!'

Come on, Dad, thought Aidan. *Come on ...*

'Yes, but it's a *huge* pothole,' said Emmi, edging round to block Berryman's field of vision.

Nearly there ...

'Practically the Grand Canyon,' said Jon, who, Aidan noticed, couldn't help gazing at the car. 'We could open it to tourists and charge an entrance fee.'

Berryman narrowed his eyes a little, looking suspicious, then he spun his head round and peered towards the stables.

Aidan exchanged relieved glances with his friends. Dad and Ann had made it.

'Pothole!' Berryman muttered. 'This car's got high-tech suspension and state-of-the-art engineering!' He settled himself back in his plush leather seat.

'I need to talk to your father,' he told Aidan. 'But you'll do. An important politician friend of the family is coming to visit ahead of the festival, and his daughter is an experienced rider.'

He revved the engine. 'I need Centurion saddled up for her right away.'

Aidan saw Emmi raise her eyebrows at him in alarm. He stepped forward, thinking fast. 'But you know how

Centurion is. Only Dad can ride him. He says he's too headstrong. I'm never allowed to handle him alone, unless he's tied to the chariot or whatever.' His voice trembled a bit. 'What if your friend's daughter was thrown off and broke her leg? Or worse?'

Berryman didn't reply. He ran his fingers through his hair then gave an irritated sigh.

'Tell your father to get another horse ready then instead, please,' he said impatiently. 'Tell him to buff up the saddle and give the horse a brush up as well – make it look its best.'

Aidan gave a nod. He glanced at Jon, who was giving him a thumbs-up. 'I'll tell him.'

Berryman revved the engine. Then he looked hard at Aidan, wagging a finger.

'But it's *Centurion* I want in the chariot race; make sure your father knows that.'

Aidan's stomach twisted.

'I'll have some important guests watching,' said Berryman, 'and Centurion is by far the fastest of the lot.' He shifted into gear. 'I don't want them to think I've given them a bad betting tip!'

The Porsche swung round the three friends and shot away with an aggressive roar.

4

CHARIOT

'Steady, Firefly. Steady.

'Ready, you guys?'

Jon and Emmi bunched closer to Aidan on the raised platform of the chariot and gave him a nod. Aidan lifted the reins and the horse broke into a gentle trot, pulling them in a circuit around the field.

'High-tech suspension!' exclaimed Jon, mimicking Berryman's voice.

'State-of-the-art engineering,' giggled Emmi.

Aidan felt himself relaxing a bit. It had been a good idea of Jon's to try out the chariot. He admired the two large wooden wheels turning smoothly; its curved, waist-high metal sides, open at the back; the long wooden struts in front that the horse was hitched to.

'Modelled on the ancient British Celt's machines of war,' said Jon with a satisfied grin. 'Welded from recycled pieces of the bonnet of my grandad's old VW Beetle.

Wheels from a cannibalised mountain bike.' He gave a happy sigh. 'Who needs a state-of-the-art Porsche?'

'Hey, Aidan,' said Emmi as the chariot started another circuit. 'If we get Firefly working really well, we can convince Berryman she's the best choice this year; make him forget all about wanting to race Centurion.'

Aidan looked at her doubtfully. 'Maybe.'

He traced his fingers over the paintings that their artist friend, Emmi's cousin Robbie, had put around the top edge of the chariot. Drawings of the 2,000-year-old legend of Queen Boudicca.

There was Boudicca in her chariot, galloping into battle with her daughters either side of her. There were her Iceni warriors clashing with Roman soldiers. Then Boudicca's body being taken to her treasure-laden tomb.

The design was all colour and movement. Robbie was a genius.

They slowed to a stop by a shed. It had an open tool-box beside it, and a collection of paint pots and jars of brushes soaking.

'Good old chariot!' said Emmi, jumping down and patting the side. 'Winner of the Carrus-under-Hill chariot race three years running, thanks to Aidan at the reins!'

'No way can we let those Roman chariots win!' said Jon,

getting out and reaching into the toolbox. He tightened the number plate with a screwdriver: *AD61*. 'Romans versus Celts. History's got to be put right once more! And this year I'm going to be filming the whole thing from the air – aerial video footage straight from my flying drone!'

Aidan smiled at Jon, unbuckling the horse from the chariot and letting her free, but he felt a prickle of worry. What was going to happen when Berryman found out Centurion wasn't pulling the chariot?

'Wheels need a bit of attention,' Emmi said, taking out a wire brush and scrubbing at the scuffed blue paint.

'Let's add some blood splats,' suggested Jon. 'Give it that authentic battle feel.' He used a chisel to lever the lid off a tin of red paint. 'And why don't we put a few speed flames along the bottom?' He grinned mischievously in Aidan's direction. 'How about spooky blue?'

'I know what I saw, Jon!' said Aidan, giving him a mock punch on the arm. He looked towards the lake. 'The fire was right there on the water.'

'I believe you, mate,' said Jon. 'Honestly! I don't think you imagined it or anything.' He dipped a brush in the tin and dabbed the wheel spokes with paint. 'So, assuming it *wasn't* reflected sunlight like your dad said – and assuming you're not a complete nutter –'

Emmi stopped her work and gave a little gasp. 'There *is* another explanation.'

Aidan looked at her.

'The way the flames appeared and then vanished like that.' She took a breath. 'Well ... what if they were *will-o'-the-wisps*?'

Jon threw back his head and laughed, then he saw Emmi frowning and stopped quickly. 'You're being serious?'

'Course I am!' said Emmi, getting a site up on her phone and reading from the screen. 'Listen to this ... *will-o'-the-wisp ... phosphorescent, ghostly light seen hovering or floating at night on marshy ground ... Many believe these ghostly apparitions are spirits not at rest.*'

Jon rolled his eyes. 'Oh man! OK.' He got a site up on his phone. '*will-o'-the-wisps are thought to result from the combustion of natural gases. Methane gas seeps occur in many places in the UK, sometimes dating back centuries* ... See? Everything can be explained by science, one way or another, Emmi Parker.'

'*When the flames of the will-o'-the-wisp were seen,*' persisted Emmi, her eyes widening, '*it was thought that someone was going to die.*'

'Yes, *me*,' grinned Jon, 'of *disbelief*!'

He spun away as Emmi swiped at him with her wire brush. 'Ven zee flames are seen ... ' Jon put on a Dracula voice. 'Many a lonely and unvary traveller has been led to their fate, never to be seen again; following zee *flames of doom*!'

He broke into a high-pitched laugh.

'Science can't explain everything, Jon Clegg!' Emmi told him.

'Come on you two!' Aidan smirked. He dabbed his brush at the wheel spokes. 'Come and help me paint some pretty, dainty blood splats, will you?'

'Lovely!' came a voice from behind them, and Aidan spun round to see Robbie standing there, holding a see-through carrier bag full of chocolate bars, crisps and cans of drink.

'Not quite up to your artistic standard, Robbie,' said Jon.

'Just the person we need!' cried Emmi, leaping up to give her cousin a hug.

Robbie emptied the bag on to the grass. 'Food,' he said. 'I seen you working. I been in the woods.'

'Collecting your special treasures again, Robbie?' Emmi said fondly. 'Getting ideas for your drawings?'

Robbie's hazel eyes lit up. He rummaged in the leather bag strapped across his patchwork waistcoat.

Aidan smiled at Emmi as they watched him. Robbie had been ill as a child; he'd got some kind of virus. He was twenty-three, and he and Emmi were really close.

Robbie brought out a higgledy-piggledy collection of his finds. He fanned out glinting feathers in his fist. 'Magpie,' he told them with a serious nod. Then he held up a piece of reddish fur and dangled it in front of Jon's face. 'Squirrel tail.'

'Nice,' said Jon, leaning back and sneezing.

'Shrew's skull,' Robbie said proudly, placing the tiny white object on Emmi's palm.

'Amazing,' she said, peering at it.

'Here.' Robbie tapped Jon's shoulder. 'Look!'

Robbie thrust what at first glance looked like a small white stick into Jon's hand.

'Hare's leg bone,' Robbie said proudly.

'You really have a thing about bones, don't you?' said Jon, with a slightly strained smile. 'Yes,' he nodded as Robbie beamed at him. 'Very nice.'

'My treasure,' Robbie said to himself quietly as he packed the objects carefully away. 'Got a fox jaw for Alice.' He blushed a little, smiling, looking down at his feet.

Emmi winked at Aidan. They all knew Robbie had a soft spot for their teacher, Miss Carter. They'd been friends since childhood, and he often took her presents.

Jon patted Robbie on the back. 'I would go for the feathers, if I were you.'

They continued to work on the chariot; Aidan coating the axle with thick layers of paint, trying to brush away the worries that kept cramming his head.

It was dusk before they finally finished.

'There!' Jon tapped the wheels of the chariot, and then ate a Mars bar in virtually one bite. 'Fit for an Iceni warrior, or what?'

Emmi gave a satisfied nod.

'Best lock her up safe,' said Robbie.

'And the chariot too,' Jon added cheekily, dodging a slap from Emmi.

They hurried to tidy up the stuff they'd been using, slotting brushes in jars of turps and sealing the lids of paint pots. They all helped to push the chariot back into the wooden shed.

'I tell you, Aidan,' said Jon, 'even without Centurion pulling the chariot, it's a done deal! Extra suspension. Increased tyre traction. You'll win the race by miles!'

There was movement on the road that ran alongside the field. People in the lane.

'The anti-fracking meeting!' said Emmi. 'We should get going.'

Jon did a theatrical yawn. 'What's the point? What we need is revolutionary action!' he said with a mischievous glint in his eye. 'Storm number 10 Downing Street.'

Then he dropped the dramatics and sighed. 'There's no point going to boring meetings, if you ask me. The government's already made up its mind. It's going to take a miracle to stop Enershale now.'

'Miracles happen,' said Robbie with a mysterious smile.

Aidan eyed him. 'What do you know that we don't, Robbie?'

The young man just shrugged. 'I've got a best treasure,' he said. 'Wait and see.'

'Well,' Emmi linked her arm firmly through Jon's with a smirk, 'whether you like it or not, we're *all* going to the meeting. Help me, Robbie!'

Robbie grinned and got Jon in a headlock. The three of them started across the field in the direction of the museum, staggering and laughing, he and Emmi pulling a protesting Jon between them. 'No, please, not the *meeting*! I'll do anything – please! Not the *community meeting*!'

'INTO THE BATTLE,' Emmi began. *'INTO THE TOMB.'*

She marched in time to the familiar Carrus chant.

'FOLLOW QUEEN BOUDICCA MEETING HER DOOM.'

Robbie joined in with gusto.

'RECOVER HER BONES FROM THE ROMAN FOE.'

Aidan started to follow them as they strode ahead, but

then he paused and glanced back, his attention caught by something.

Firefly and Fenland Queen were a little way off, pressed close together, making strange, low snickering sounds he'd never heard before.

'HIDE THE TOMB WHERE NONE DARE GO!'

Aidan stretched out a hand and tried to approach them, but they were too jumpy to be touched.

'LAY HER TO REST IN A TOMB OF HER OWN,

'LAY HER TO SLEEP ON HER FINAL THRONE!'

Shadows from the trees of Carrus Woods crept over the field, making dark purple patches. Overhead, clouds collected, as if a storm was on its way.

'What is it?' he called to the horses.

A breeze lifted their manes. He saw them toss their heads; eyes wide, staring towards the lake. Faint swirls of mist lingered over its surface.

'ETERNAL SLEEP, FOREVER IN YOUTH.' His friends' voices sounded further away now. 'GUARDED BY LEVERETS, VALOUR AND TRUTH.'

What was it? Aidan peered into the gloom. His heart thudded.

'BURY HER BONES ... '

Two figures were standing by the bank of the lake.

'BURY HER SWORD!'

Two girls. Tall like Emmi. Side by side. Completely still.

'IN A STONE-CARVED TOMB, WITH A ROYAL HOARD!'

There were whooping cheers and claps.

The figures vanished.

'You coming or what, Aidan?' Jon hollered through the dusk.

'You go ahead,' Aidan shouted in their direction. He stared hard at the place where he'd seen the girls.

Maybe Jon was right, he thought as he scanned around the lake; maybe he was a nutter after all. 'I'll catch you up!'

'OK.' There was the sound of chatter; Jon making a joke; loud laughter; then his friends' voices faded.

It must be the stress of Centurion and the prospect of the move, thought Aidan as he gave a final glance round the lake. Maybe it really was all getting to him way too much. Messing with his head.

He was about to turn to go, but then caught his breath.

Close to where the figures had been, there were two flames on the water.

He gaped.

Flickering, shifting shades of blue.

Aidan's body tensed as he watched them. He thought about shouting for Emmi and Jon, but they were long gone, the fields around him deserted. He pulled out his phone and tried some shots, but the camera wasn't working and when he typed Emmi a message, there was no signal to send it.

Aidan swallowed, mesmerised by what he was seeing.

The blue flames had started to move across the lake. One glowing brighter, then fading; the other taking turns to glow brighter, then fade. They travelled across the water and into the meadow.

A pair of flames, they moved like footsteps across the grass.

Daring him to follow.

5

WILL-O'-THE-WISPS

Aidan tracked the blue flames as they moved across the meadow and on to the dark lane beyond.

'I can't believe I'm doing this,' he muttered to himself. 'It is way too freaky.

'Zee will-o'-the-wisp,' he croaked quietly. 'Come to lead me to my doom.'

The flickering lights led the way along the narrow road and towards the edge of Carrus Woods, and the museum. Lights from the main hall spilled through the tall, narrow windows of the building where the meeting was being held.

But why was he being led here, Aidan wondered?

He went up the gravel driveway, weaving between the parked cars, and approached the front.

The will-o'-the-wisps glimmered briefly by the main entrance, and then disappeared.

Aidan slipped inside and paused in the foyer. He could hear voices coming from the hall. Echoey coughing and low conversations told him there was a roomful of people; a discussion in full flow. No sign whatsoever of the blue flames now.

'Fracking pollutes water and can cause earthquakes,' someone was saying. There was a round of applause and Aidan tiptoed towards the room. The door was ajar and he peered in.

Inside, people filled the rows of chairs set out between the exhibition cases and along the old dark wood panelling of the museum. He saw the backs of Jon, Emmi and Robbie. James Berryman was strutting about at the front, in a baggy tweed jacket that looked like it had belonged to his dad. *Typical of Berryman to put himself in charge.*

Aidan's eyes were drawn to a movement. The flames were back, rising up the wall at the far side of the hall, out of sight of the others, overlapping and intertwining over a low doorway.

To reach them, Aidan realised, he'd have to cross the whole room without being seen; somehow slip between the display cases behind the back row of chairs. The last thing he needed was to be spotted by Berryman.

He took a long breath and eased the door wider.

'The environmental risks are exaggerated by the media.' Berryman's reedy voice. 'Enershale follows strict safety regulations in order to operate – do you think I'd lease them my family's land if they didn't?'

There were loud grumbles from the audience. One person called out. 'You're only pro-fracking because of all the money you're making out of it!'

Aidan stepped inside the room.

'We're talking jobs for the people of Carrus!' Berryman ignored the comment, his voice stretching over the din. 'A secure energy future for this country!'

And our future? wondered Aidan as he took another step. *New school, new flat on the seventeenth floor. Definitely no horses allowed.*

He reached the safety of the closest display case and crouched behind it. Through the glass he saw Roman coins and spear tips set out on dusty red velvet.

'And a secure payout for you, Lord Berryman!' Aidan's drama teacher, Miss Carter, called.

Aidan had made it halfway across the floor. The eerie flames were swirling faster now, as if they were beckoning him more urgently.

'Carrus has a rich historical heritage, as this museum proves,' came a voice Aidan recognised as Mr Williams. The elderly museum curator stood up, resting a hand on the back of his chair for support.

Ahead, Aidan saw another glass cabinet, the last one before the doorway he was aiming for. Inside was a stuffed hare standing up on its back legs, the fur threadbare, bristled into uneven clumps. Aidan found his gaze drawn to the animal. It seemed to fix him with huge amber-coloured glass eyes.

Aidan shook himself. He looked again at the flames and noticed that they seemed to be getting fainter. *Get a move on!* Crouching, he started to cross the space towards the case ...

'*Exhibits,* is that what you call them, Mr Williams?' Berryman said. 'A mangy stuffed rabbit, for goodness sake! I've seen better specimens on my Sunday dinner table!' He broke into his donkey-like laugh.

There was a ripple of laughter in return. Mostly grunts of disapproval. Aidan dived behind the exhibition case as heads turned backwards to look at the hare.

He knelt there, peering through the glass of the cabinet.

'The *hare* is the noble emblem of Carrus-under-Hill.' Williams' voice quivered in indignation. 'The royal symbol of Queen Boudicca.'

The blue will-o'-the-wisps still played along the frame of the doorway, almost within touching distance. Aidan waited for the right moment to make a dash for it ...

'I for one believe the old stories,' Miss Carter told the hall. 'There's no doubt in my mind that the true site of the last great Iceni-Roman battle was right here in Carrus.'

Her words made Aidan catch his breath, though he wasn't sure why. He snuck a look and saw her stand up with a swish of her flowery skirt, turning to face the audience. She swept her long, blonde hair into a clip with a determined expression. The room was very quiet; the only sounds muffled wails of the wind blowing outside; uneasy gusts rattling the windowpanes.

Berryman was gazing at her, his mouth slightly open.

Miss Carter's bracelets clinked together on her slender arms as she raised them. Her large blue eyes flashed.

'Boudicca's tomb *is* here,' she said with authority. 'Somewhere. We just haven't found it yet. And it's a total disgrace to allow fracking when a national treasure of such importance could be right under our feet!'

The audience broke into cheers and applause.

Aidan gave a muffled cry.

The case with the hare in it ...

He stumbled back, struggling to keep his balance ...

There had been a woman's face reflected in the glass.

A face.

Pale, and still as stone.

Grey-green eyes staring straight at him.

He somehow made it through the doorway, shrinking into the shadows behind it.

The applause inside the hall continued, the sound blurring in his head as he tried to control his panic.

The clapping subsided, but Aidan stayed fixed to the spot, heart racing, his mind still filled with that face.

The woman had been familiar somehow; but where had he seen her before? He tried to remember, but couldn't.

'Queen Boudicca's tomb,' Aidan heard Williams repeat Miss Carter's words dreamily. 'It's almost too much to hope for; finding the tomb would certainly stop the fracking for good. It's likely the whole Carrus area would be declared a World Heritage Site.'

Berryman's braying laughter. 'Yes, that might just do the trick! Discover the final resting place of the most iconic warrior queen in history. Good luck!'

'Get a grip, will you?' Aidan muttered to himself. First the phantom flames, now phantom faces. Things were just getting weirder.

He took in his surroundings. He was at one end of a long corridor. High, round windows cast shafts of murky twilight down into the space. No will-o'-the-wisps in sight. There was only one direction to go in from here.

He headed towards the dark doorway at the end of the hall.

EXHIBITION ROOM, read a wooden sign, pointing the way. And below it, a printed notice:

DONATE YOUR HISTORICAL OBJECTS.
HELP CARRUS FIND ITS LOST TREASURES
AND HALT THE FRACKING.

DEPOSIT ITEMS IN CASE, WRITE YOUR NAME
ON SUPPLIED CARD, CLICK LID TO LOCK.

Aidan moved down the corridor. This call for artefacts sounded like a bit of a desperate measure to him. The idea that someone had been keeping a priceless Iceni artefact to themselves for years but might suddenly donate it to the museum was a bit hard to believe.

But then, Carrus *was* desperate.

'We need more archaeological surveys of the area,' Aidan heard Williams' voice echo. 'This is the driest summer on record, and the drought conditions we have just now would be perfect for more aerial studies, which can be excellent for spotting potential sites.' The curator gave a heavy sigh. 'But many months, not to mention thousands of pounds, would be needed to investigate every mound and every hollow.'

The discussion faded into the background.

Aidan slowed his pace as he approached the doorway.

In front of him, the space filled suddenly with blue light.

6

THE SHADOW MAN

Aidan's hand instinctively reached out towards the will-o'-the-wisps. He felt a fascinated shiver in his fingertips and the flames dissolved away in smoky blue strands.

There was the scraping of chair legs from the hall as people stood up to leave; the murmur of conversation. From outside came the sound of footfalls on the gravel drive. Car engines rumbled to life; headlights swept across the walls of the corridor from the high windows.

'Anybody left in the museum?' Mr Williams' voice called out from the hall, some minutes later.

Aidan stayed quiet. There was no way he was leaving until he'd tried to work out why the flames had led him here.

He heard the entrance door slam. A key in a lock. There was the eerie sensation of being completely alone in a big old building full of history and secrets.

Heart thudding, he stepped into the exhibition room.

Aidan waited a few seconds, letting his eyes adjust. He decided that it was best not to turn on the light; someone might see from outside. Through the gloom he made out the shapes of display cases, most of them empty. So much for people donating their priceless treasures.

Aidan moved silently between the cabinets. The few objects inside them didn't look much different from what was in the main hall: crooked Roman coins and broken arrowhead blades mostly, with white cards alongside with information about what they were; definitely not the kind of treasures to stop Enershale in its tracks.

Aidan froze.

He'd heard a noise from the other side of the room.

Footsteps.

The hairs on the back of his neck prickled as he listened hard. There was definitely someone moving about over there. Why hadn't they answered when Mr Williams had called out?

Aidan crouched behind the nearest case. His breathing sped up. Had whoever it was heard him come into the room?

The noises continued; muffled scuffling; a sound like metal scraping wood.

Aidan strained to see through the shadows. There was someone – a man? – by one of the cases. A thin beam of torchlight flitted about, but never caught the person's face. There was a sudden sound of glass breaking and scattering. Then a bang, and moonlight spilt across the floor as the fire escape at the far end of the room was flung open and the figure disappeared through it.

Aidan rushed to the door and looked out. But the drive was deserted. There was no sign of anyone in the lane.

He went back inside, fingers scrabbling along the wall for the light switch. He flicked it a few times, but nothing happened.

He got out his mobile, turning on the torch so that it cast a glow across the room and its rows of cabinets. He moved cautiously forward, his foot crunching on something, and he shone the phone down to find the shards of glass covering the wooden floor. Running his phone light up from the ground, he saw a smashed display case. It was empty.

An unsettling creaking punctured the silence as the fire escape swung to and fro on its hinges.

Aidan peered more closely at the cabinet. Jagged pieces of glass still sat in the frame. He noticed blood spots on the floor – a trail leading towards the fire exit. Whoever it was must have cut themself.

Aidan shone his phone into the broken case. As he inspected it further, he realised that the cabinet wasn't completely empty after all.

Carefully, he extracted a piece of white card. He put his phone close and saw that the paper had something on it. He peered at the text, recognising the handwriting immediately.

DONATED BY ROBBIE PICKERSGILL

Robbie.

Aidan remembered his mysterious comment when they were by the chariot; what was it again? *I've got a best treasure. Wait and see.* Was this what he'd meant?

What had been inside the case? Aidan wondered. What was so important that someone would want to steal it? Should he phone the police right away? He had to tell the others about all this!

He rattled off a series of quick texts to Jon:

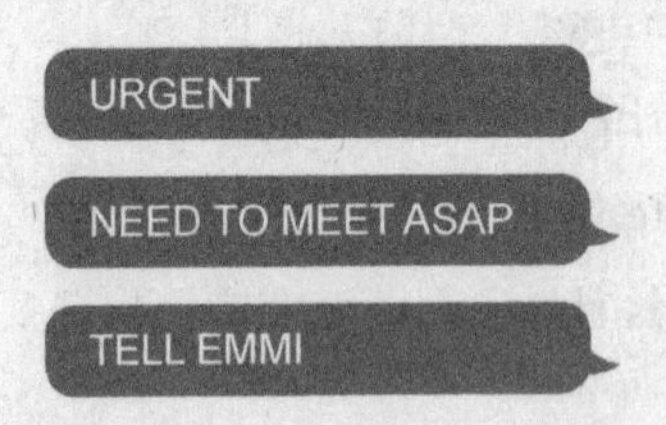
URGENT
NEED TO MEET ASAP
TELL EMMI

And that's when Aidan smelt the smoke.

7

FIRE

Aidan turned to see flames licking up the far wall. Smoke curled like black tongues over the old wood panelling of the museum. It was shocking how fast it was spreading, greedily gobbling the dark varnish with a spitting crack.

Aidan stared. An acrid smell hit the back of his throat. Coughing, he shook himself into action. He looked for the fire alarm and sprang towards it, smashing the flimsy round pane of glass.

Nothing.

Nothing?

He hammered it again with his fist, but no bell rang out.

The smoke was getting thicker fast, swirling forward to fill the spaces between the exhibition cabinets. A case nearest the fire already had cracks spreading and widening across it from the heat. Before he could react, the glass exploded, and Aidan crouched, shielding his face as jagged pieces flew across the room.

He lowered his hand from his eyes, thoughts tumbling. It crossed his mind to save some of the artefacts. He thought about Mr Williams, and Miss Carter, and all these objects collected over years and years. Should he try and make a mad grab?

But there was no time. Already the glass of another case had soot coating it in a speckled brown film; cracks webbing through its surface.

Flames circled the doorway to the corridor. The smoke got denser. Aidan took wheezy breaths. His head became fuzzy, as if he was starting to faint.

Have to get out.

He tried to get to the open door leading outside, blinking hard to see the way, eyes streaming in the sooty, suffocating atmosphere.

He sank down, chest flat to the floor, gulping at the clearer air and pulling himself forward. He became disorientated by the smoke. He tried to listen for the creaking of the open fire escape, hearing nothing except the rushing crackle of the fire.

Aidan groped around. He smelt a waft of cooler air and scrambled towards it; tumbling and rolling on to sharp stones – gravel – swallowing air into his lungs.

His vision was still blurry. Strange shadows flitted over

the driveway in the firelight. There were shapes; figures on horses; strange sounds mixed with the growl and hiss of flames. A noise like galloping hooves that couldn't be real; high-pitched neighing.

There was a wave of heat at his back. An army of flames.

The blaring wail of a siren blotted out these sounds; a strobing blue light made the scene vanish.

Aidan stumbled away from the blazing building. Black soot coated the insides of the museum windows, and there were more explosions of glass as the panes shattered. There was the crash of timber falling, sparks and leaping light.

A police car screeched to a stop near him and the door was flung open.

An officer got out. 'What's the story here, son?'

The rest all happened so fast. An ambulance arriving; a fire engine thundering along the drive, throwing up gravel like shrapnel; a medic looking Aidan over and giving him the all-clear. That same police officer in conversation with someone from the fire brigade; the two of them looking over in his direction.

The policeman headed towards Aidan.

'Get in the car, son.'

'What?' Aidan backed away a step. 'Why?'

'Just get in the car.' Aidan noticed the handcuffs

dangling from the policeman's waist; his hard stare of suspicion.

'I want to know why,' Aidan said. His heart beat fast.

'You are being arrested for arson,' the policeman said matter-of-factly. 'You have the right to remain silent.'

Aidan gave a gasp. 'But I had nothing to do with it!' he stuttered.

'We have an eyewitness statement,' the policeman went on. 'Someone saw you acting suspiciously at the back of the hall during the meeting.'

'Who told you that? It wasn't me!' Aidan insisted. *Wasn't this policeman listening?*

The officer pointed at the open door of the police car. 'I won't ask you again.

'Get in.'

A spear plunges towards them. One horse rears, blood spraying from its neck. A high-pitched neigh that is more like a shriek pierces the air. The chariot swerves, tilts. The three are thrown to one side, clutching at the reins, at the air.

8

BATTLE PLAN

Aidan breathed in the smell of fresh hay and leather tack, filling his lungs with the comforting, earthy aroma of horses.

But from outside the stable door, carried faintly on the warm morning air, was the stale smell of burning.

Aidan shivered and zipped up his jacket.

Arson. They'd accused him of starting the fire. He still couldn't take it in.

He watched Ann the vet listening to Centurion's chest with a stethoscope, Dad stood nearby with a brooding look.

'Aidan, are you OK?' Emmi burst through the stable door, breathless. 'We heard what happened!'

Jon was with her, his eyes wide. 'I can't believe they think you did it!'

'It's total madness,' Dad muttered. He caught Aidan's eye, but then looked away, and Aidan got a queasy feeling. Did Dad *really* believe that he had nothing to do with the fire?

After all, he hadn't believed him about the flames on the lake.

It was obvious the *police* hadn't believed his story about the person he'd seen. Things the officer at the station had said shunted through Aidan's mind: *Look, Aidan, there's no evidence anyone else was involved. We know you've been having some family issues: your mum's illness; you having to leave Carrus for your dad's new job ...*

Aidan's hands had tensed into fists. All of that was none of their business!

Other things he'd been told flashed through his head: *You are going to be released on bail and are ordered to appear in court next week.*

It looked bad – Aidan knew that – him creeping around the museum after it was closed. But what was he supposed to tell the police about what he was doing there? Following ghostly will-o'-the-wisps that nobody else could see? That really would get him locked up!

And then there'd been the hallucination, or whatever that was; the shadows of galloping horses; the thunder of hooves; the terrified neighing.

No, he'd kept his mouth well and truly shut about both of those things.

For obvious reasons.

The vet unplugged the stethoscope from her ears and ran a hand slowly along Centurion's leg. The horse made a rumbling noise deep in his throat.

'There are signs of an infection,' Ann said. 'I can give antibiotics, but I've got to say the wound isn't healing as fast as I'd hoped.' She rooted around inside her leather bag. 'There's no way he can be seen by Berryman, or it'll be obvious something's up.'

'But the race is tomorrow!' cried Emmi. 'Berryman wants Centurion to pull the chariot!'

'There's absolutely no chance of that,' said Ann. She gave Centurion another injection.

'And if Berryman comes looking for him?' said Emmi.

The question hung in the air, unanswered. Aidan glanced at Dad, but he was standing motionless, still lost in his own thoughts.

'Aidan,' Emmi said quietly, 'are you coming to today's protest? Fracking starts tomorrow evening during the festival and ... '

'Haven't you heard?' frowned Ann, snapping the clasp on her bag shut. 'The fire triggered a clampdown. The police are panicking about an escalation in public disorder and they've come down hard. The protest camps were dismantled this morning and there were quite a few arrests.'

Emmi gave a gasp of dismay. '*What?*'

Aidan signalled to her and Jon and the three of them went outside.

He quickly filled them in on everything that had happened – all the details of the fire and the theft.

'The stolen object was donated by *Robbie*?' Emmi quickly messaged her cousin on her phone. 'Are you sure? Did you tell the police that?'

'I couldn't see the point,' Aidan told her, 'especially when it was obvious they didn't believe me about someone else being there and smashing the case.'

'We should keep that information to ourselves anyway,' Emmi said hurriedly. 'At least until we've had a chance to talk to Robbie.' She tried another message. 'Oh, he's still not answering!'

'What do you think Robbie meant,' said Aidan, 'when he said he'd found a *best treasure*? It must be what he donated to the museum, right?'

'Well, it couldn't have just been one of his animal skulls or some old bones,' said Jon. 'Not if someone took such a lot of trouble to steal it.'

'Nobody can prove anything was even stolen.' Emmi twisted a strand of hair between her fingers. 'There won't be any record of what was in the museum case, with people just going in and donating stuff when they wanted. Do you still have Robbie's card, Aidan?'

Aidan shook his head. 'I lost it in my rush to get out.'

'Well, whoever stole Robbie's object, that same person also started the fire!' Emmi said with conviction.

'To cover their tracks,' she explained, as Aidan and Jon stared at her. 'Think about it: all the glass cases were broken in the heat and everything was destroyed. If you hadn't gone in there, Aidan, no one would have even known about the theft.'

'Makes sense,' said Jon, slowly nodding. 'Whoever it was probably thought the museum was empty. And you said the fire alarm wasn't working, Aidan?'

'They would have disabled it!' said Emmi. 'So the place would be a total inferno before the fire brigade got there.'

'But what was so important that someone was willing to destroy a whole building?' said Aidan.

'Whoever it was must have had a really good reason,' Emmi said. 'They didn't want anyone to know what was in that case.'

She tried Robbie on her mobile again. 'Where *is* he?' she muttered. 'You know what it's like when he's in the middle of his wanderings or working on an art project. He's probably roving about the lanes somewhere with his sketchpad and has left his phone at home. Oh, we *so* need to talk to him. *Right now!* We've got to clear your name, Aidan, find out what's behind all this!'

'And on the other minor subject of *the fracking starting tomorrow evening*?' said Jon. 'And Aidan having to move away if it does?'

'Yes,' said Emmi, 'how are we going to stop the fracking? The protest is virtually dead – you heard Ann. So we need another tactic.'

'Easy!' said Jon glumly. 'All we have to do is find Queen Boudicca's tomb and get the whole Carrus area declared a World Heritage Site before teatime tomorrow evening – just like Mr Williams said. Easy as hot cherry pie, and a cold can of Coke!'

He licked his lips. 'Man, I'm thirsty.' He pulled at the neck of his T-shirt. I wish this heat would ease off a bit.'

'I saw that storms are forecast for tonight,' said Emmi. 'The dry weather's going to break.'

Emmi's words caused a memory to shunt into Aidan's mind. He gripped Jon's arm a bit too hard and his friend flinched. 'What was that other thing Mr Williams said in the meeting?' he asked hurriedly. 'Something about the drought?'

'What? Well,' said Emmi, frowning as she tried to

remember, 'he was saying this is the driest summer on record ... and then he was talking about archaeological surveys ... and he said something about the drought conditions being perfect for ... '

'Aerial studies!' finished Aidan. A plan was forming as he remembered Jon's idea to film the chariot race from the air.

His thoughts whirred. It was crazy. Crazy, but irresistible. His fingers twitched, as if he was charged up with a strange kind of electricity. He pulled up Google on his phone and scanned through some sites. Maybe it was the adrenaline of being arrested; of being a suspected criminal, wrongly accused. Maybe it was being so worried about Centurion. Maybe it was because of being forced to move away. All he knew was that he *had* to do *something.* Determination sprang up inside him like hot little flames.

'We are going to find Boudicca's tomb,' he announced.

'What?' Emmi raised her eyebrows. Jon stared at him.

Whatever it took, thought Aidan; however impossible it was.

They had to – find – Queen – Boudicca's – tomb.

And he had a plan of how to do it.

His friends shuffled closer as he started to explain the strategy.

By the time he'd finished, Emmi's eyes were gleaming with excitement. She had her phone out as well, scanning sites that had more of the information they needed. 'If it's here to be found, we *are* going to find that tomb, Aidan,' she said firmly. 'We won't let you lose your home without a fight.'

'No way, Aide!' added Jon. 'We'll do everything we can to help.'

Aidan felt a rush of emotion at his friends' words. 'Thanks guys.'

'I feel obliged to delicately point out that the odds are not exactly in our favour, though,' said Jon. He shook his head. 'Less than thirty-six hours left. Nothing to go on. Experts like Williams have spent their entire lives searching for Boudicca's tomb and drawn a blank. You'd have to be a total nutter to even try.'

He broke into a grin as he fist-bumped Aidan.

'Count me in! Operation Tomb Boudicca is *go*!'

Part 2

Into the battle,
Into the tomb,
Follow Queen Boudicca
Meeting her doom.

Recover her bones
From the Roman foe,
Hide the tomb
Where none dare go.

Lay her to rest in a tomb of her own,
Lay her to sleep on her final throne.
Eternal sleep, forever in youth,
Guarded by leverets, Valour and Truth.

Bury her bones,
Bury her sword,
In a stone-carved tomb,
With a royal hoard.

9

OPERATION TOMB BOUDICCA

Aidan watched Jon lay the green canvas bag at the top of the small sunlit hill overlooking Carrus Woods. A few clouds drifted lazily across an otherwise blue afternoon sky. No sign of the forecast storm.

'Perfect flying conditions,' said Jon happily.

His voice went down a notch. 'Ready?'

'I really think this is going to work!' Emmi said eagerly.

Jon began to unzip the bag, then grabbed his friends' arms and pulled them close, as if he was about to break the Official Secrets Act.

'*Remote-controlled drone,*' he hissed.

Emmi gave an appreciative gasp as Jon reached into the bag.

Aidan's skin tingled. This was it. The only sure way they had to sweep a big area, mega fast.

They'd spent all morning researching everything they could on archaeological aerial surveys. What they'd read confirmed what Mr Williams had told them about drought conditions increasing the chances of finding something. They'd learnt what patterns to look for on the dried-out ground: unexpected coloured lines or shapes only visible from the air that could mark out something below the surface.

'State of the art,' Jon said proudly, laying the drone on the brown-tinged grass.

Aidan probed the odd-looking contraption. It was like a kind of squashed helicopter, black in colour, with four sets of propellers on the top to get it airborne. The whole thing rested on an arching pair of metal landing skids, and fixed underneath was a digital camera.

Jon sat back, looking very pleased with himself. 'Primed and ready to fly,' he said with a small salute. He pulled a laptop from the bag.

Aidan's heart beat faster. There was so much resting on whether they could stop the fracking – so much more besides protecting the land: his dad's job on the estate, their home, Centurion ... did they really have a chance of finding anything?

Jon lifted up a remote-control box.

The rotors on the drone started to turn with a whirring sound, quickly gathering speed until the blades were a blur of movement.

Aidan watched him tap the computer keyboard and an image flashed up on the monitor.

'The camera and the laptop are talking to each other,' Jon said with satisfaction. 'We have live film footage. Take-off at my command.'

He clicked a button and the rotors sped up.

'Good to go?' he asked over the buzz.

Aidan gave a nod. This was really it. The search for Boudicca's tomb was on!

He saw Jon tweak the small joysticks each side of the control box with his thumbs, and the drone rose smoothly into the air and hovered over the ground like some kind of robotic insect. The computer screen was filled briefly with a smiling Emmi giving the thumbs up, then all Aidan could see was the ground behind her as the machine climbed.

'Nice and easy,' Jon said to himself. 'We don't want any sudden, crazy movements.'

The drone dipped unexpectedly, doing a noisy sweep right over their heads. Emmi gave a shout as Aidan ducked.

'Just testing the aeronautics!' Jon laughed. 'OK,' his face became serious. 'Get watching the screen you two. I'm taking her higher.'

The drone lifted away again, moving quickly towards the woods.

'We're looking for any unusual patterns,' Emmi reminded Aidan as they knelt together by the laptop. 'Watch that tree, Jon!'

'Woah! Emergency manoeuvre!' Jon tilted the control box forward as the screen filled with a view of leafy branches.

The drone continued its flight, beaming back images from the camera. Aidan got an aerial view of his house, then the sprawling building of Berryman's mansion surrounded by its ornamental gardens; the meadow and lake, the stables. How was Centurion, he wondered?

OK, concentrate. He glued his eyes to the monitor.

The yellow-green rectangles of the fields filled the screen like patchwork. Narrow channels crisscrossed along them, glinting in the few places where water was still running through. He saw a red car speeding along one of the lanes.

'Anything yet?' called Jon.

'No,' said Emmi. 'Head towards Carrus itself.'

There was the village green, and the car park by the pub, the blackened shape of the museum ... Jon had his tongue sticking out between his teeth as he flew the drone. 'Let's take the sweep further out.'

The drone became a moving dot in the distance; so far

away that Aidan could hardly hear it any more. He peered at the screen, seeing more fields, the odd house, patches of trees – but nothing out of the ordinary as far as he could tell.

As time ticked by, Aidan started to get uneasy. He'd been so sure they'd have found something by now. He'd been so full of hope when he'd come up with his idea, but it was never going to be that easy, was it? If it were, surely someone would have found something long ago.

Emmi glanced at Aidan. 'We've still got loads of land to survey,' she said, giving him a lopsided smile. 'Can we try east now, Jon?'

'Affirmative,' said Jon. He made adjustments to the control box, head bobbing down at the computer to check the flight path.

A siren sounded in the distance.

'Nothing there,' said Emmi. 'Take her up a bit more.'

On the screen Aidan saw flashing blue lights in one of the lanes.

Jon frowned, squinting at the monitor. 'There's an ambulance.' He zoomed in with the drone camera.

Aidan's breath caught. 'There's someone lying in the road.'

He felt Emmi grip his arm. He saw her eyes widen as she spoke.

'And they're not moving.'

For a moment, time seems to stop. The twisting horses. The girls grasping air. A gold-black Roman banner fills the sky; an eagle with its wings outstretched.

Then the chariot overturns.

10

ROBBIE'S BEST TREASURE

Everyone on the bus was talking about it.

The hit-and-run on one of the lanes near Carrus that afternoon.

A man, knocked down by an unknown driver.

Left for dead.

Robbie Pickersgill.

'Is there any news, sweetheart?' Aidan could hear Miss Carter's strained voice on the end of Emmi's phone as their bus headed towards the hospital. 'They won't tell me anything.'

Emmi was sitting next to him, looking very pale. 'He's still really poorly.' She bit her lip. 'The hospital told us he woke up for a short while but he couldn't remember anything about what happened.'

'Oh, love.'

'The police are appealing for witnesses, but ... ' Emmi blew her nose. 'They said he's lucky to be alive, Miss.'

Aidan saw Jon hang his head.

'Well if there's anything at all I can do,' Miss Carter sounded like she was trying hard not to cry. 'Anything at all. All you have to do is ask, you know that, don't you?'

Aidan stared out of the window as Emmi hung up. On his knee was a drawing pad and a tin of sketching pencils; presents for Robbie. The evening shadows clung to the buildings on the outskirts of town. He still couldn't take in what had happened.

Emmi twisted a friendship bracelet round and round on her wrist. 'He was out with his sketchbooks, I bet,' she said, the words coming out in a rush. 'Must have been – that's why he wasn't answering my messages. He was always looking for new inspiration for his art. Maybe he was into a new drawing and standing too close to a bend and the car didn't see him in time. He wouldn't have heard it coming and – '

She stopped talking and stared at her lap.

Jon turned to them, running a hand through his hair. 'Dunno,' he said. 'But why didn't the driver stop the car and help him? Maybe whoever it was panicked.'

Emmi gave a hard little shake of her head. She was quiet a few moments and then leaned in, lowering her voice.

'What if the driver was *deliberately* trying to murder Robbie?'

Aidan and Jon stared at her.

'I think you must be in shock, Em,' Jon said nervously. 'Er ... *murder*?'

Emmi's hands fluttered about. 'It's too much of a coincidence, don't you think? Robbie's mystery object gets stolen from the museum, and the next minute there's a fire.' Her voice dropped even further, to an anguished whisper. 'The following day he's knocked down and left for dead in a hit-and-run.'

Emmi put a hand to her mouth and her eyes went wide. 'And what if whoever tried to kill him comes back to finish the job?'

Aidan found himself slowly nodding.

'You definitely watch too much telly, Em,' said Jon with a shaky laugh, but Aidan thought he looked pretty worried.

'We have to *do* something!' insisted Emmi. 'Find out what's going on.'

'But why Robbie?' Aidan held the back of Jon's seat. 'Everyone likes him. He hasn't got any enemies. If *only* we'd taken more notice when he was telling us about his special treasure.'

'None of us took enough notice,' said Emmi sadly. 'But we all know what a hoarder Robbie is, and that his stories can be a bit far-fetched ...

'Oh, Robbie!'

The bus approached the hospital. Emmi leapt up and pressed the stop button. 'We have to know if he's OK, that's the first thing.' Aidan felt the bus slow. 'And then we have to ask him exactly what it was that he donated to the museum.'

'They might not let us see him, you know,' said Jon as they waited by the door. 'Even if he is out of intensive care, he might not be conscious.'

They filed out of the bus. It had dropped them right opposite the hospital, a grey high-rise building with a strip of trampled lawn and a token scrubby rose bush, without any flowers.

They told the receptionist at the front desk who they were there to see, and she called over a tall male nurse to talk to them.

'I'm very sorry, but you can't see Mr Pickersgill now,' the nurse said. 'He's resting.'

'But I'm his cousin!' Emmi pleaded. 'It would only be for a few minutes.'

The nurse shook his head. 'Not even family are allowed in. Visiting hours are very strict, and other patients need their peace and quiet.'

'Robbie's in a room of his own, though, isn't he?' Emmi persisted. 'Number twenty-nine on the fifth floor, my parents were told. So we wouldn't be disturbing any other patients if we go and see him.'

'No,' the nurse said firmly. 'I'm sorry. You'll have to come back tomorrow.' He went striding off in the direction of the wards, enormous, white plastic Crocs squeaking.

Aidan pulled the others away from the desk and they huddled by a vending machine. 'What now?' he hissed.

'We've got to make a dash for it!' said Emmi. 'When no one's looking.'

'Are you serious?' said Jon.

A doctor went past, deep in conversation on his mobile, and the three of them pretended to be choosing snacks from the machine.

Aidan sneaked a look along the long corridor the nurse had gone down. Squeaky Shoes had disappeared. 'Let's go!'

'We shouldn't be doing this, guys,' said Jon as they rushed towards the lift.

'Shush!' hushed Emmi. 'And keep a look out!'

There was an anxious wait for the lift, before the three could slip inside.

'Fifth floor,' muttered Aidan, pressing the button.

The lift travelled upwards and came to a stop. The doors slid open and Aidan peered out. 'All clear!'

They headed down a corridor, moving quickly and

pausing at the junctions.

'Hostile nurse at three o' clock!' Jon hissed.

They sprang back, pressing themselves against the wall.

Squeaky Shoes squeaked past.

'Where did *he* come from?' said Jon shakily.

'We've got to be quick,' Aidan said, scanning the room numbers above the row of doors. 'He could be back any time.' He ran a few paces further on. 'Here it is!' he beckoned. 'Room twenty-nine.'

Aidan hesitated a moment, breathing hard. His fingers curled round the door handle ...

Maybe they shouldn't be doing this after all. Maybe Robbie really did need to rest, and it was wrong to go disturbing him.

But this was urgent.

Aidan pressed the handle and eased the door open ... then stood there staring.

He heard Emmi give a little gasp; Jon catch his breath.

Robbie was lying on a bed by the window. Narrow shafts of light came through the slats in the blinds. His face was so bruised, Aidan hardly recognised him. His lips were puffed up and his eyes were closed and ringed by nasty purple bruises. There was a tube taped to his neck, and another one on his arm that went to a drip suspended by the side of the bed. A monitor next to him pulsed in time to his heartbeat, a green line spiking rhythmically.

Aidan swallowed. He quickly closed the door behind them and put the presents – the pad and pencils – on to a chair.

The three friends edged nearer.

'Robbie?' Emmi whispered. She took hold of his hand. 'Robbie. It's me, Emmi.'

Robbie shifted in his sleep. He murmured fitfully, like he was having a bad dream, and Aidan saw his eyes flicker under their swollen lids.

Aidan took Robbie's other hand. He decided it might not be the right moment to tell him anything about the museum being burnt to a crisp and his special treasure stolen. 'This is Aidan, Robbie,' he began uncertainly. 'Er, I saw a card with your name in one of the cases ... at the museum.'

The word was like some kind of magic trigger.

Robbie's eyes snapped open. He looked at them with startled eyes that couldn't seem to focus.

'Robbie!' Emmi exclaimed. 'Thank goodness! We've been so worried.' She clutched his hand. 'What did you donate to the museum, Robbie? Can you tell us?'

Robbie levered himself up with a grunt, grimacing with pain. He was trying to tell them something, but his swollen mouth was making it too difficult for him to talk.

He strained to reach the sketchbook on the chair.

Jon grabbed the pad and tore off the plastic, flipping to the first page and handing it over. 'Here Robbie – take this, mate.'

Emmi prised the lid off the tin of pencils, pressing one into her cousin's left hand.

Robbie began to draw.

Aidan saw his fingers shaking, but he was amazingly fast, the pencil almost a blur over the thick cartridge paper as he sketched.

The three of them drew in closer to watch, mesmerised.

Aidan saw a round shape appear on the page, then on it a horse ... no, two horses. A pair of horses pulling a chariot, three figures riding inside.

The picture grew in intricacy; it was of an engraved band of some kind. *What is it?* Aidan asked himself. *A piece of jewellery?*

'It looks like an arm bracelet,' whispered Emmi. 'It's amazing.'

Footsteps sounded in the corridor outside and Aidan glanced worriedly at the door.

Robbie continued his drawing, adding detail to the other side of the bracelet. This time it wasn't horses, but some other kind of animal ...

The footsteps were getting closer. Shoes squeaking.

'Hurry!' hissed Jon, all the colour drained from his face.

A sprinting shape with gem-like eyes materialised on the page.

'A hare!' said Emmi quickly. She clasped her hands together, mouth wide with astonishment. 'But a hare – that's the symbol of Boudicca!'

Excitement prickled through Aidan. 'Where did you find it, Robbie?' he asked urgently. He heard the beeping of Robbie's heart monitor speed up. '*Where?*'

The footsteps were right outside the room. There were voices now as well. That tall male nurse who'd told them to stay away.

Robbie let go of the pad and pencil and gripped Aidan's arm, making him cry out in surprise. The heart monitor beeped louder and faster.

'Our secret ... ' Robbie managed with his swollen mouth, his breathing all wheezy. His voice was strangely youthful sounding, as if it was a little boy speaking rather than the Robbie they knew.

'Tree roots ... like snakes ... '

Robbie held Aidan's arm even tighter. He sounded terrified.

'Bones ... through the gaps ... Can't take those bones!

'Got to leave those kind of bones where you find them. Wouldn't be right!'

Robbie's eyelids fluttered as he struggled to keep them open. 'Someone's trapped me,' he whimpered in that child-like voice. 'Down here in the dark. Can't ... can't get out!'

Aidan felt Robbie's grip slacken. 'Trapped where, Robbie? Where were you when you found the bracelet?'

The door handle was turning.

'*Where?*'

The door was opening.

But Robbie had slumped back on the bed, his eyes closed.

The door swung wide with a whine. Jon gave a little yelp.

The nurse filled the doorway.

It took a few seconds for the man to register what he was seeing. First his face went a waxy white like his Crocs, then a stormy shade of red. His chest expanded alarmingly as he filled his lungs with air.

'OUT!' he bellowed. '*OUT!*'

'Sorry!'

'Sorry!'

'Sorry!'

Aidan scooped the sketchpad off the bed and the three friends slipped round the nurse and tumbled out into the corridor, breaking into a run.

11

THE DISCOVERY

'So much for *Mr Pickersgill needs peace and quiet*,' mumbled Jon as he stood back on the little hill with the drone remote control.

'We *were* breaking the rules,' Emmi told him, as she and Aidan stared hard at the laptop screen. 'What did you expect? We just need Robbie to get better. Oh you *have* to get better, Robbie!'

The sun was low in the sky, sending out weak light over the landscape. Dark clouds were gathered on the horizon, and a fresher wind had picked up.

'Storm coming,' muttered Aidan. He watched the buzzing drone flying in the distance with a tinge of anxiety.

He thought about the sketch. That horse-drawn chariot. That leaping hare.

A hare.

The symbol of Queen Boudicca.

'We'll find something this time,' said Emmi determinedly. 'The arm bracelet is the best proof we've had that Boudicca was at Carrus!'

'Too right!' Jon agreed.

'It's evidence that Boudicca was buried in this area, I'm sure it is,' Emmi went on, 'and that our legend in the Carrus chant is true – we *so* need to know where Robbie found it!'

'Well there's no way we'll be allowed back into that hospital to ask him any time soon,' said Jon. 'We'll have been banned from that place for life!

'But why didn't Robbie tell us about the bracelet sooner?' he asked, adjusting a dial on the remote control. 'That's what I don't get. Why the big secret when he knew how important it was?'

Emmi shrugged. 'You know what Robbie's like. Last-minute surprises are his style. And technically, it's a *torque*,' she added, matter-of-factly as she studied the drone's-eye view on the screen. 'That's what you call that kind of arm bracelet. It would have been worn at the top of the arm.'

'Those things Robbie told us,' said Aidan, keeping his eyes fixed on the images that were being projected back. '*Tree roots like snakes. Bones through the gaps* – that was creepy. And about being trapped in the dark ... what did he mean, do you think?'

Emmi shook her head. 'Don't know. He's never said anything about that to me before. Mum and Dad have never mentioned anything either, but I don't want to ask them – they're worried sick as it is.'

She frowned. 'It sounds like something happened to Robbie when he was younger; something that really scared him ... Head south Jon; we've scanned that area already.'

Aidan glanced worriedly at his watch. Those grey storm clouds were moving closer. If it rained, any aerial patterns that were to be found in the dry landscape were going to get messed up.

'*Unusual coloured lines or shapes on the ground,*' recited Emmi. 'Come on drone! *Come on!*'

'Take her higher,' Aidan said. 'We need to check the fields by Miss Carter's house.'

His phone gave a sharp beep and he pulled it out of his pocket to read the text.

From Dad.

His heart sank as he read the message:

Sorry Aidan. On train to city. Last minute issue with the new flat needs sorting. Back first thing tomorrow.

Arranged for you to stay at Emmi's tonight.

Ring you later.

'Tomorrow?' Jon gave a whistle as Aidan told him and Emmi. 'What if he's not back in time for the chariot race? When Berryman sees you hitching up Firefly and not Centurion ... ' He shook his head. 'His reaction won't be pretty.'

'Don't remind me,' Aidan replied. Without Dad around to help him deal with Berryman ... he felt sick just thinking about it. He tried to focus his mind on the job in hand.

'Last area coming up,' Emmi warned.

'We are recording all this, aren't we?' asked Aidan.

'It'll all be there,' said Jon, 'stored in the laptop.'

Aidan stayed glued to the screen, willing something to appear.

'Progress report?' called Jon after a while.

Emmi shouted at the air in frustration. 'Nothing! That's five square kilometres we've surveyed now!'

'The battery on the drone's only got a few minutes of charge left,' said Jon. 'He shifted his thumbs on the controls. 'I think we need to bring her back to base. Mission abort.'

'No!' Aidan protested as the drone came quickly towards them and hovered over their heads with an angry-sounding buzz. 'Look at that sky – it's bound to rain!'

'You can't stop now, Jon!' agreed Emmi. 'Any patterns there might be will get washed away. Send it out one last time,' she insisted. 'There's still some power.'

'And if she's a hundred metres in the air when the battery gives up?' said Jon. 'You realise that's goodbye drone, for good?'

'Just one more time, Jon,' begged Aidan. 'Please!'

Jon gave a sigh, then turned back to the control box. 'I don't like to say it,' he mumbled as the drone quickly gained height again, 'but maybe there's a simple reason why all the other aerial surveys around Carrus up to now have drawn a blank.' He glanced at them. 'It's because there's nothing to find.'

'This is the biggest drought since records began,' Emmi reminded him defiantly. 'If there's something to see, then it's going to be now.'

'Energy levels critical,' Jon said grimly. 'Back en route to target.'

The drone swept away from them over the landscape and Aidan stared hard at the shots projected back from its camera. The low sun sent the long shadows of trees towards them. Memories pulled at the back of his mind; a strange jumble of images and sounds.

He remembered other shadows; those shadows on the grass in the firelight as the museum burned. That high-pitched wail of dying horses ... He saw Centurion lying injured in the meadow ... remembered running and running through the woods for help.

Below the drone, a creature made a twilight dash across a field.

Aidan thought about the hare in the museum case and the woman's face he'd seen overlaid on it. Those grey-green eyes looking straight at him. Her silent stare trying to tell him something ...

And in that moment Aidan remembered.

He remembered where he'd seen that woman before.

'Carrus Woods!' he cried out, leaping up to grab Jon's arm.

'What?' said Jon. The drone swerved dangerously and he gripped the box to bring it back under control. 'The battery's in the *danger zone* guys.'

'We've not scanned Carrus Woods itself!' Aidan's heart hammered as the wild idea came to him.

'But it's all trees,' said Emmi. 'If the tomb's in there, we'll never have a chance to see any markings on the ground and – '

'It's not all dense trees though, is it?' Aidan persisted.

There was no time to tell them about the woman in the clearing who'd disappeared when he got close to her; how it had been *her* face he'd seen in the museum case as he'd followed the will-o'-the-wisps. All he knew was he was caught up in something he had to be part of now.

'Out of time, guys,' said Jon through gritted teeth. 'I've got to bring the drone down *right now.*'

'Sweep the woods, Jon!' cried Aidan.

Emmi caught Aidan's excitement. 'Pass over the woods, Jon – that's an *order*!'

Jon gave a deep sigh. 'Commence suicide mission,' he muttered.

Aidan glanced at the drone as it moved sluggishly out over the trees. The laptop screen filled with branches and leaves. And then ...

'*Houston, we have a problem!* I've a red flashing light, guys,' said Jon. 'I won't be able to land her in that lot. *Please* tell me you see something!'

The drone wavered. There was a chugging, spitting sound as it dipped dangerously low towards the canopy.

'Mayday, mayday!' Jon called as the drone struggled away from the woods. 'We're going down! Emergency landing!'

The machine managed to clear the trees and fell ominously towards an adjacent field below the hill they were standing on. It pitched, then plunged, making ragged bounces along the ground as it fell, twisting over and over in the air. It came to a crunching stop, upside down.

'Dronie!' wailed Jon. 'My beautiful dronie!'

Emmi turned away from the screen and looked at Aidan, eyes alight. She clasped his arm and he beamed back at her, knowing she must have seen it too ...

Just before the drone had been pulled away from the trees ...

Slap bang in the middle of Carrus Woods ...

Jon looked at them, then sprang down to kneel in front of the laptop, hammering at the keyboard. 'What did you see, guys? What did you see?'

The aerial video zipped backwards. The three friends pressed in close to watch as it played the last ten seconds.

Jon hit pause and stared, his mouth hanging open.

Aidan felt a ridiculous wave of hope. *It might not mean anything*, a nagging voice in his head said. *Don't build your hopes up too much.* But he couldn't help grinning stupidly all the same.

This was what they'd been searching for.

A sign.

Their one chance.

The frame on the computer screen showed a clearing, just visible in the fading light. It was the same clearing Aidan had passed through on his way to the demonstration; the place with that massive old horse chestnut tree with the twisting roots; the spot where he'd first seen that woman.

And there, where the summer heat had dried up the ground ...

There was a circle.

A perfect circle where there shouldn't be one.

A band of dark gold etched out in the parched earth.

Emmi grabbed Jon's arms and danced about with him on the hilltop.

'We'll need to take torches, right?' she said drawing to a breathless stop, the words tumbling from her mouth. 'It's getting dark so quickly with these clouds coming over. I'll go back for some, and something to dig with too. I'll tell Mum and Dad we'll be out late; I'll think of an excuse.' The wind blew her hair, so there was a wild look about her. 'We need to get out there before the rainstorm hits.'

She looked at Aidan, her face full of curiosity. 'How did you know to look in Carrus Woods itself?'

'I'll explain on the way,' said Aidan, quickly helping Jon pack the laptop and remote control into the canvas bag. 'I'll drop your stuff off at my house,' he said, zipping up the bag and slinging it over his shoulder. 'I've got to give the horses their last feed anyway – check on Centurion. Meet back at the stables everyone. Fast as possible!'

Jon gave a salute and headed down to retrieve the

mangled drone. He turned back and punched a fist in the air. 'Target identified!' he shouted, and Aidan gave a laughing holler in reply:

'Tonight's the night we find Queen Boudicca's tomb!'

All is screaming metal and splintering wood. The white gleam of bone through quivering skin; a horse's lips drawn up against its teeth.

The woman's sword is near her on the ground and she draws it from its sheath with an angry cry. She heaves herself across the ground with it, as the soldiers come closer. The leaping hare along its hilt sparks in the sunlight; its ruby eye flashes. She grips her royal daughters with bleeding hands, whispering urgently to them.

12

BY THE LAKE

Aidan patted Centurion and the big horse nuzzled against him in the gloomy stable. But the animal was agitated, moving away from him the next moment with a snort.

Fenland Queen and Firefly were acting strangely too, standing pressed together in the next stall, jittery and wide-eyed, stamping their front hooves. They slurped a bit of water from the bucket Aidan offered them, but then Firefly tipped it up. When Aidan offered them each a handful of their favourite oat mixture from the barrel, they tossed their heads at it, blowing the flakes back at him.

Aidan sighed, his worry swinging back to excitement as he thought about getting to the clearing.

The clearing!

Sweat prickled his skin. A brisk, humid breeze was blowing, the kind you get when a storm is on its way. The wind whined through the chinks in the stable roof, rattling hinges and window panes. Centurion's ears were laid back flat, and he ground his teeth, looking towards the entrance as if he sensed something out there in the twilight.

'It's just the wind, Centurion.'

Was it though?

Torchlight flicked under the gap in the door, sending shadows scurrying up the walls.

Jon and Emmi? Aidan's heart skipped a beat.

The door creaked open, and the shape of a figure loomed up the wall. A head appeared. Aidan gave a gasp as he saw the whites of a pair of eyes and a gaping mouth.

'You ready Aide?' said the mouth.

'Jon?'

The face grinned and Jon gave the thumbs up. As well as a black balaclava, he was wearing a camouflage jacket complete with combat trousers and black gloves.

'I like the gear, Jon-Boy,' said Aidan.

'Can you please take that thing off your head?' said Emmi, coming into the stables. 'You look like you're going off to rob someone!'

Jon sighed and pulled off the balaclava so that his mop of hair stuck up in all directions. He'd painted combat stripes across his cheeks. 'Just want to look the part, Em. Night manoeuvres and all that.'

Emmi opened the flap of the rucksack she was carrying and tossed both of them a head torch. 'I've also got three super-strong trowels for digging.'

Aidan smiled at Emmi's organisation. He fixed the torch on his head and twisted it on. 'We need to get going.'

'Straight across the meadow is the fastest way,' said Jon, dazzling them with his lamp.

They set out, their lights jumping about as they hurried from the yard, strands of mist caught in the beams.

They passed the shed where the chariot was, and Aidan saw that the wind had blown the doors wide open. The Iceni costumes on their rail fluttered about like headless ghosts, and his eyes glanced at the chariot's designs as he bolted the doors shut: Boudicca drawing back her bow, her daughters either side of her. Dead bodies lying twisted round the wheels of their chariot.

He had an image of Robbie, lying there in his hospital bed, and Aidan's teeth clenched in anger. Who could have done that to him? How was the arm bracelet involved?

They got to the meadow. The mist was thicker here. The clumps of gorse bushes looked like hunched, scuttling creatures in the moving torchlight.

Aidan came to a sudden stop.

He angled his light beam at the ground and stared

towards the lake. Emmi and Jon moved closer to him, so that all three of them were pressed up against each other. He heard Emmi's fast breathing.

'You can both see them this time, right?' he whispered.

Jon gave a low whistle, then a shaky laugh. 'So it wasn't all just a figment of your warped imagination after all, Aidan!'

'Will-o'-the-wisps!' Emmi gasped.

'The combustion of marsh gases,' corrected Jon, but he didn't sound at all sure any more.

Two blue flickering columns of fire rose from the lake, quivering and slowly twisting, moving to settle on the bank.

'No way ... ' said Jon. Because now, in place of the flames, lit by a blue glow, there were two figures.

Aidan stood there, mesmerised.

They were the same two girls he had seen there before, side by side, absolutely still, looking right in their direction.

'Who are they?' Emmi whispered by Aidan's shoulder and he felt her shiver. 'I don't recognise them from the village. What are they doing just standing there like that?'

The worried snorts of the horses carried from the stables. 'Let's go and talk to them,' said Aidan.

The others nodded shakily and the three of them slowly approached the figures.

The two girls still hadn't moved. Now that they were nearer, Aidan could see that each of them had some kind of cloak wrapped round her; one with fur along the edge. The other had a long reddish plait coming down the front of her shoulder almost to her waist. They were both still looking right at them. *At him?*

Aidan felt their stares; a connection that he couldn't understand.

'They're beautiful,' Emmi murmured. 'But they look so sad.'

Aidan felt a few spots of rain on the top of his head. 'You two OK?' he called, not really sure what to say. 'You lost?' he added falteringly.

Aidan got close and the girls continued to stare, their grey-green eyes wide; their skin very pale. The hairs on the back of his neck prickled. They were mouthing words but no sounds seemed to be coming out. They lifted their hands.

'They're trying to tell us something,' said Emmi. 'Who are you?' she called to them, managing to keep her voice steady.

A shower started; the surface of the lake became peppered with drops, ripples spreading over its surface. There was a sound like a hiss of breathing, then the rain started, pelting hard. Droplets slid down Aidan's wind jacket and dripped off the hem as he hurriedly pulled up his hood.

Water poured over the dry surface of the meadow baked by weeks of sun, unable to seep into the hard ground, flowing towards the steep banks of the lake.

'They're not ... ' Aidan heard the fear in Jon's voice as he lifted a finger to point. 'I know this sounds freaky, guys, but those two are not getting wet!'

Aidan gaped at the girls. It was true. While his, Jon's and Emmi's clothes were already virtually saturated, the two girls were unchanged by the teeming rain; as if the water was passing round them, through them.

'That's just not scientific,' mumbled Jon, taking a step back.

Aidan shivered.

'Who ... ' began Emmi, her voice filled with an intense curiosity. '*What* are they?'

The answer hung in the air between the friends, but none of them wanted to voice it.

There was a lightning flash; a jolting thud of thunder and Jon gave a small cry.

The girls held out their arms in a sudden sweeping motion, and as their cloaks fell behind them, Aidan saw that each had a bracelet on her upper arm – a wide golden band.

Lightning flashed again, sparking off the metal.

Aidan felt an elbow in his side. 'That jewellery,' Jon hissed, 'looks exactly like Robbie's sketch!'

The girls pointed to the edge of the water, at the soggy earth the run-off was pouring over. They cupped their hands, their faces frowning. They made urgent gestures, their mouths moving silently.

In a moment, Emmi was on her knees, leaning forward to dig.

'They want us to search the bank!' she cried, pushing the wet hair out of her face. 'That must be it! Come on you two!'

Aidan didn't stop to wonder why. There was no time to ask questions. On impulse he sprang forward to join Emmi and scraped up handfuls of muddy soil.

'The water level's rising!' he spluttered as the rain ran down his face and neck.

Whatever it was they were searching for, they only had minutes to find it, he realised. Soon the bank would be submerged under dark, silty water.

'Here!' cried Emmi, throwing open the flap of the rucksack and rummaging inside, then tossing them a trowel each. Aidan hacked at the soil.

Jon was by his side. 'We need to dig faster!'

Aidan sliced into the compacted surface, again and again. The tool bent out of shape and he threw it down, resorted to using his hands. His fingers were already freezing. His fingernails were clogged up and his knuckles throbbed.

By their ghostly torchlight, the three of them gouged and dug as the rain pounded the bank, crumbling it into dense clods as parts of it eroded away in the rush of water.

Aidan swatted his eyes. It was getting even tougher to dig, and they'd found nothing. The slick mud of the bank became more viscous and difficult to shift.

The water rose higher.

'There's nothing here!' Jon shouted over the lashing rain, and the wind and the thunder.

'Keep looking!' insisted Aidan.

He glanced back at the girls. Their bodies flickered strangely – transparent, blueish, as if they were made of flames. With a jolt, he realised that they were fading.

Time was running out.

Aidan could hardly feel his fingers any more, but he continued to grab at clods of earth with as much force as he could.

His head torch was virtually dead now, and he was

working mostly by touch, his hands scooping at the flooded bank. The water level was up to his armpits as he reached downwards; the clay solidifying like cement.

'It's impossible, man!' Jon shouted.

Aidan's teeth chattered. Now the girls were little more than pale blue outlines, as if their energy was all spent, dying away to nothing. He felt himself slipping against the slick surface of the bank, about to tumble forward into the water. He made a desperate swipe ...

And felt something solid against his numb fingertips.

Aidan caught his breath. He scraped at the edges of the object.

Whatever it was, was wedged. Stuck fast.

'Help me!' he grunted at Emmi and Jon.

All three of them crowded round the spot, prising and wrenching.

There was a movement. A slight shifting.

'Again!' shouted Aidan and they gave a frantic tug.

The hard object came free and they fell back on to the grass behind them in a splash of water.

Aidan was sodden and bone cold, but he lifted the object triumphantly, and his friends mouthed a cheer. It was covered in a thick layer of cloggy mud so there was no way to tell what it was.

All he knew was it was heavy. Unexpectedly heavy.

He looked around for the two girls, but they were gone.

'Mission to extract the mud ball ... ' Jon panted, rain teeming down his face, 'accomplished.'

'Let's get to my house,' Emmi said between gasps. 'Clean it up.'

Aidan nodded, and the three of them hurried away through the storm.

13

THE PAST UNEARTHED

'Ah,' Emmi's dad said mildly, looking up from his laptop as the three of them tumbled into the warm kitchen. 'You're a bit mucked up,' which Aidan considered the understatement of the millennium.

Jon sneezed. His face was so covered in mud he looked like he had his balaclava on. 'Might need to get a bit of a wash, yes,' he blinked.

Aidan stared at his own dirt-splattered face in a mirror. He was still in an excited daze. He thought back to the two girls and the mysterious object cradled in his bulging anorak pocket. He eased the coat off and wrapped the nylon material into a bundle.

'What've *you* got there?' said Emmi's dad, giving the soggy parcel a prod.

'Er ... we got caught in the storm, Dad,' said Emmi quickly, ignoring his question and easing herself between her dad and Aidan. She pulled off her jacket and dumped it on the mat. 'OK to sort this out later?' She nudged Aidan and Jon towards the stairs. 'You know the boys are staying tonight? We're pretty hungry actually.'

'Excellent!' Emmi's dad rubbed his hands together then unhooked a pan from a nail on the wall. 'For supper we have duck pâté and ravioli with spinach and ricotta, then marmalade roll and custard ... '

Aidan's mouth watered. He realised he was ravenous.

'Yes count us in for all of that!' called Emmi. 'We'll clean up.

'I'll let the boys borrow some of my clothes,' she added, getting a horrified look from Jon.

They rushed upstairs and locked themselves in the bathroom, Aidan quickly unwrapping the muddy mass from his anorak and laying it in the sink.

Emmi and Jon crowded round to see.

'Ready?' he asked.

Aidan heard the rain drumming on the window. He took a breath. 'Right.' His hand trembled a bit as he reached for the tap. 'Here goes.'

'Not too hot!' Emmi warned. 'We don't know what we're dealing with here, or how delicate it is.'

Aidan turned on the water and began to rub gently at the layers of sludge. Brown water filled the basin as the dirt fell away.

'Guys,' Emmi said after a while, as she watched Aidan work. 'What just happened out there?'

Jon gave a nervous laugh. 'Don't ask me!' He dipped his fingers under the tap and rubbed at his face. 'I'm still recovering from the idea of having to wear your clothes.'

'They were *ghosts*, weren't they?' said Emmi in a hushed voice. 'We saw *ghosts*!'

'Those two girls were pretty ... out there,' Jon said shakily. 'Pretty weird. They could have been ... or maybe ... ' His shoulders slumped.

'Ghosts,' he said helplessly. 'Definitely ghosts.' He gave a weak grin. 'Think of the hits we could have had on YouTube if we'd got video footage.'

Aidan smoothed away more mud. 'But why would ghosts appear to *us*?'

'I don't know,' said Emmi, her eyes wide. 'They're not at peace – '

'Or maybe they just get a kick out of scaring people to death,' said Jon. 'Not that I was petrified out of my skin, or anything,' he added quickly.

'You think we should tell my mum and dad?' said Emmi. 'They might have ideas about what all this means – '

'No way!' interrupted Jon.

Aidan shook his head. Under his fingertips he could feel the hard surface of the object as the silky mud got washed away.

'No,' he said. 'I agree with Jon. We can't tell anyone else, Emmi. We have to keep this between just the three of us for now. We don't even know what we've found yet.'

Aidan thought about the girls as he cleaned up the object, the intense way they'd fixed him with their stares. 'I've no idea why, and I know all this is crazy ... but those girls chose us. They're trying to tell us something.'

'We are ... *the chosen ones*!' croaked Jon.

'Well we *are*!' said Emmi. 'Aidan's right.' Her eyes glinted. 'This is the most freaky, amazing thing that's ever happened to me!'

'Woah!' Aidan blinked hard.

The centre of the muddy ball had fallen away in a clod, leaving a wide, round hole. He rubbed more cautiously.

A gold colour glinted under his fingers and he heard Emmi catch her breath.

He saw engravings appear: a horse ... two horses, pulling a chariot – three figures riding inside.

'Oh my god,' Emmi whispered.

Aidan washed away the last of the earth and lifted the object up.

'It's amazing!' she cried softly. 'An arm bracelet. Just like the one Robbie drew!'

'Hang on.' Aidan quickly dried his hands, got the sketch from his pocket and smoothed out the damp piece of paper.

'No.' he inspected the torque closely, comparing it to the drawing. 'It's similar, but not exactly the same. Look! Both have the same chariot design, but see the hare? On the drawing it's *sprinting*.' He raised the golden armband. 'Here the hare's *standing up on two legs*.'

'You're right,' nodded Emmi.

She gripped Aidan's shoulder. 'Do you remember the ghost girls' jewellery? Weren't their torques just like these?'

'Yeah,' said Jon slowly. 'They were.'

'Do you realise what this means?' Emmi danced about the bathroom. 'This bracelet could be enough! That's what Robbie meant about miracles do happen. A hare is the symbol of Queen Boudicca. It *totally* proves that she had a connection with this area; and that the legend is true. Boudicca really is buried round here with all her treasures!' Bottles of shampoo and shower gel went flying. 'It's bound to stop the fracking and spark a major archaeological survey! All we have to do is show this torque to Mr Williams and Miss Carter and ... '

Aidan held on to her arm. 'Wait, Em! Slow down!'

Emmi stopped moving and looked at him.

Aidan frowned. 'If we tell anyone about this, the news will be round the village in no time'. His eyes darted to the window and he lowered his voice.

'If someone did try to kill Robbie – they're still out there. If they find out we've got a bracelet almost identical to the one they stole from the museum, they could come after us next.'

'Ah. You're right,' Emmi said, fiddling with the corner of the hand towel. 'Course you're right.'

She put a hand to her mouth. 'Do you think Robbie is safe in the hospital? I mean, we got into his room easily enough, and that means somebody else could. Maybe we should just go straight to the police and tell them everything we know; about Robbie drawing the sketch for us, and ... '

'Aidan's in enough trouble with the police, don't you think, Emmi?' interrupted Jon. 'He's got a court case next week! And how's it going to look if they find out he's been trespassing inside a hospital ward?'

Jon shook his head. 'No. We just have to hope the hospital have stepped up security after that nurse found us in there.'

The glass of the bathroom window rattled with the force of the rain. Aidan looked at their three worried faces reflected in it.

'We have to find the tomb,' he said determinedly. 'By ourselves. In secret. Get to the truth of all this.'

His two friends nodded back at him from the glass. 'Soon as the storm eases off,' he said, 'we go to search that clearing.'

'Meanwhile ... ' said Jon turning to Emmi. Delicious smells were wafting from the kitchen and Aidan's stomach growled. 'Tension makes me hungry. Do you think there's any chance your dad's got supper ready yet?'

'I'll ask,' said Emmi. 'And meanwhile, we need to do loads of research about Boudicca and Carrus and the battle with the Romans – see if it gives us any clues to what's going on.'

She led the way from the bathroom to her room. 'Can we please have our food up here, Dad?' she called down the stairs. 'We've vital homework to do and can't be disturbed. It's a matter of life and death!'

'Sure, darling,' came her dad's cheery reply. 'Happy to help avert disaster.'

Emmi flopped on to a beanbag with her laptop. 'Get googling on your phones you two and let's see what we can find out.' She started to type. 'I'll go for will-o'-the-wisp sightings in this area.'

Jon rolled his eyes at Aidan. '*Bossy*,' he mouthed, but got quickly to work, sitting cross-legged on the bottom bunk bed. Emmi's dad came in with a trayful of food, smiled at the three, all absorbed in their screens, and left again.

Emmi tapped her computer screen. 'It says here that will-o'-the-wisps date right back to Celtic times.' She swallowed a forkful of pasta. 'Ancient Britons worshipped the places they appeared.' She shuddered. 'There's evidence that Romans might have used such dips in the ground as fire pits for human sacrifices. How horrible!'

'There are several sites where it's thought Boudicca's last battle against the Romans could have taken place,' said Aidan, absent-mindedly smearing pâté on a cracker.

'I've got the British Museum archive up here,' said Jon. He got a big spoonful of marmalade roll and custard as he read from the monitor. '*An authenticated Roman account translated from the original Latin.* Woah!'

'What?'

'Cool weapon!' he munched. 'Listen to this: "*Foes fall back when the wild queen wields her sword; the formidable battle blade. A leaping hare on its hilt, its demonic scarlet eye, a huge ruby.*"'

In his mind, Aidan imagined that sword. Its gleaming silver edge; the sleek, red-eyed hare.

Emmi took Jon's phone and carried on reading. '*The symbol of the hare was allowed to be carried and worn only by the Warrior Queen Boudicca herself and* ... oh!'

She looked at Aidan and Jon, wide-eyed.

'What?'

'... *and her two royal daughters.*'

Jon's next spoon of pudding hovered in mid-air on the way to his mouth. 'So what you're saying is ... '

'Only Boudicca – *and her daughters* – were allowed to wear the hare as a symbol,' repeated Aidan, his thoughts whirring.

Jon ran his fingers through his matted hair. 'So those ghost girls we saw ... ' he said slowly. 'They have to be ... *had* to be ... ' His spoon clattered back into his bowl.

Emmi gave an excited nod.

Aidan's heart thudded.

The realisation hit.

The two girls by the lake.

They were the daughters of Queen Boudicca.

The soldiers loom over them. The girls are hauled up by their hair, kicking, clawing at silver armour and red tunics, spitting words; dragged away from their mother and towards the marsh.

To the men, the words are little more than clipped screams. Only those who speak the Celtic tongue would understand their meaning.

You break our land;
But never our people, never their power.
Let our honour be restored at the chosen hour.

14

TO THE CLEARING

It took a very long time for Aidan to fall asleep that night. His mind was buzzing with a mix of excitement and dread.

Robbie, the stolen bracelet, Centurion and the chariot race tomorrow, the fracking ... the criminal charges against him for arson seemed the least of his worries.

He lay on the bottom bunk and listened to the rain drumming on Emmi's bedroom window, and Jon's deep breathing from above.

As soon as it got light, the three of them had decided, no matter what the weather, they were going to search the clearing.

'*Meanwhile I'll hide the arm bracelet.*' Emmi's words came back to him. '*We have to keep it a deadly secret!*'

By itself the bracelet wasn't enough to stop the fracking, they'd all agreed that. And who knew what would happen if the thief got to hear about what they'd found?

The swirl of thrill and anxiety kept him awake for what

seemed like hours, and when Aidan did finally fall asleep, he dreamt of his mum.

They were in the stables together.

Mum was stroking Centurion's nose and the big horse nuzzled against her.

'Look after him, Aidan, won't you?' she said. 'Until I come back.'

'But why do you have to go away?' Aidan had replied.

'Promise me, Aidan.' Mum squeezed his hand. 'Promise me you'll look after him. Keep him safe.'

'Stay,' insisted Aidan. 'Don't go.'

Then somehow they were suddenly out in the open and a heavy rain was falling, and Mum was drenched and shivering, and he kept pleading with her not to go, but she was getting fainter and tinged with some kind of blueish light, and when he tried to catch hold of her, his hand went straight through her and there was nothing to hold on to ...

'Promise me, Aidan.' Her voice was so faint now he could hardly hear it. And he was scrambling to see where she had gone, but there was nothing but rain and cold and shadow.

'Aidan?'

Aidan opened his eyes and sat up.

'You OK?' Emmi was by his bed looking at him with a frown.

Jon was rubbing his eyes, head dangling over the top bunk, his hair in tufts. 'You were mumbling in your sleep, Aide.'

Aidan blinked at them as the room came into focus. Daylight squeezed itself through a gap in the curtains. He scrambled out of bed, hurrying to get his thoughts straight. 'What time is it?' he said. 'We need to get to the clearing!'

'Early,' said Jon. 'But it's still lashing it down.'

'We can't let that stop us,' said Emmi. She was already dressed and heading for the door, gathering items into a small rucksack on her way: the three trowels, the head torches. 'I've spare wellies for both of you.

'Now let's go!'

OOO

'Boudicca's daughters,' said Jon as they picked up the pace over the rain-sodden fields towards Carrus Woods. He opened the flowery umbrella Emmi had given him. 'I just can't work them out. Why they would appear. Now. To us.'

'Nobody knows what happened to them after the last Iceni-Roman battle,' Emmi said as they skirted a flooded patch. 'Historians don't even know their names. Imagine that – we don't even know the names of the daughters! We *do* know that Boudicca and the two of them were treated really badly by the Romans after the girls' father, the Iceni king, died. They say it was this horrible treatment that sparked off the whole revolt.'

'Yeah,' agreed Jon. 'It got the Celts really angry. And they'd had enough of being ruled over by the Romans and told what to do.' For some reason Berryman's arrogant face came into Aidan's head. 'But that doesn't explain why now. Why us.'

'I think the daughters want to help us,' Emmi said as they squelched quickly over the marshy ground. 'They've been disturbed by what's going on in Carrus. I don't think they like the fracking any more than we do!'

'Come on!' Jon rolled his eyes. He stumbled on a tussock in his oversized wellies, spraying Aidan with water. 'Why weren't the ghosts at the demo then?'

'How do you know they weren't?' said Emmi. 'Their land's in danger!' she added passionately. 'That's what I think. That's why they're appearing after all this time. Think of how they fought for this place, this land; the people they saw killed because of it – people on both sides. They led us to the arm bracelet. They wanted us to know who they are.'

'Yes,' agreed Aidan uncertainly. But he couldn't help thinking there must be more to the story.

The conversation was interrupted by a buzz from Emmi's phone, and she pulled it out to look at the message. Her face went pale.

'It's from my mum,' she muttered. 'News about Robbie ...

'He's still not conscious,' she swallowed. 'He's a whole lot worse.'

'Oh, Robbie!' she said as she read the flow of messages and hurriedly tapped back replies. She gripped Aidan's arm, so hard that it hurt.

'The doctors are saying he might not make it.'

They stopped by a low wall, standing in silence, catching their breath.

Aidan wanted to say something to Emmi, but he didn't know what. Jon was silent too, staring at the end of his wellies.

Emmi wiped her eyes. 'They're going to let the family in to see him this evening if he hasn't improved.'

On the other side of the wall was a small stone cottage, the house hemmed in on three sides by the edges of Carrus Woods. Miss Carter's house.

'Meadow Acres' said a painted plaque on the gatepost, and Aidan recognised the distinctive style of Robbie's artwork in its frame of flowers. He saw what he guessed were Robbie's presents decorating the gateposts: a piece of slate painted with galloping ponies; the rib bone of something or other; and what looked like the skull of a fox, its sharp little teeth bared.

Emmi stopped suddenly. 'Really we should go and see Miss while we're passing,' she said quietly. 'Check she's OK. You know how close she and Robbie are, being friends at school and all that. She knows how much Robbie liked her ...

'Likes her,' she corrected herself. Aidan heard her swallow and go on rapidly. 'And she'll be so upset about the museum being destroyed, especially after all the help she gave Mr Williams with the campaign and getting more artefacts and everything.' Emmi swung open the gate. 'We shouldn't stay long though.'

Jon filed through after her, but Aidan hung back.

Might Miss Carter believe the police and think he had started the fire? She was bound to have heard about the arson charges by now. He hated the thought of his teacher thinking badly of him. She'd lost her mum when she was younger, just like he had. And her dad shortly after. Aidan couldn't imagine what it was like to lose both parents.

'Just no one say anything about any of the tomb or ghost or bracelet stuff,' he told the others.

'No, not even to Miss Carter,' said Emmi over her shoulder. 'We have to keep all this secret. Remember what we agreed? Think of the danger we could put her in with Robbie's attacker still on the loose!'

Aidan followed his friends past the flower beds of foxgloves and hollyhocks, a cheery burst of colour on that wet, grey morning.

Emmi lifted the horseshoe knocker and gave three taps, and they waited for the door to be answered. There was the movement of a curtain, then the sound of footsteps inside. The door opened a chink, then swung wider.

'What a lovely surprise!' said Miss Carter. She was dressed in jeans and a white T-shirt, her blonde hair tumbling over her shoulders. She was putting on a smile, but Aidan saw that her eyes were a bit red round the edges, as if she'd been crying.

'Hullo Miss.' Jon pulled his umbrella closed, flapping the drops off and accidentally spraying everyone with flecks of water.

'Come on in.' Their teacher ushered them in and they piled their wellington boots and Jon's crumpled umbrella by the door and went into the kitchen.

There was the smell of flowers and baking bread, and the big pine table in the centre of the room was crammed with costumes and props.

'Excuse the chaos,' Miss Carter said, clearing Roman helmets and Celtic cloaks from chairs so they could all sit down. Aidan saw Iceni brooches made of silver-sprayed cardboard, eagle-decorated shields; realistic-looking bows and arrows and swords.

A painted banner was hanging across the room drying:

CARRUS-UNDER-WOODS
ICENI-ROMAN FESTIVAL
CHARIOT RACE
THIS AFTERNOON AT 5PM

This afternoon. Aidan's stomach did a somersault as he thought about Centurion and his injured leg. About Berryman expecting the horse to compete.

'All this looks great, Miss!' said Emmi. 'You always do amazing stuff for the festival.'

Miss Carter returned a smile. 'You're a sweetheart for saying so. I'm a bit behind schedule, but getting back on top of things now.' She went over to the sink and filled the kettle.

'Have you seen Robbie, Miss?' Emmi asked tentatively. 'Since the accident, I mean?'

Miss Carter shook her head and lit the gas with a match so that a little ring of blue flames flared up. 'The hospital is being very strict about letting people into his room.'

'Oh, really?' muttered Jon, catching Aidan's eye. 'I wonder why.'

Miss Carter turned to Emmi. 'Is there any more news?' she said worriedly. 'It's family only for visiting, I expect, but it's so difficult not knowing anything.'

'He's ... ' Emmi glanced at Aidan. 'He's fighting,' she said quietly.

Miss Carter bit her lip and nodded. 'If your family hears anything more, you will tell me straight away, won't you?'

'Course I will,' Emmi assured her. She sniffed.

Miss Carter handed Emmi a tissue, and Aidan saw Jon looking as awkward as he felt.

'Er, we saw the ambulance arrived really fast at least,' blurted Jon. 'I guess things could have been a lot worse if it hadn't.'

Miss Carter took a biscuit tin from a shelf. 'You saw the accident?'

Aidan exchanged glances with Emmi and Jon.

What were they supposed to say to that? Aidan felt his

heartbeat quicken. Maybe they *should* tell Miss Carter everything after all. Glancing at Emmi's face, he guessed she was thinking the same thing.

'Er ... we were messing around with my drone,' said Jon quickly, getting a chocolate digestive from the tin and practically putting the whole of it in his mouth in one bite with nerves. 'We didn't see much. Just got a bit of a view on the laptop of where it happened, and the police and that arriving.'

But Miss Carter didn't seem to have heard him. The kettle had started a high-pitched whistling as it boiled, and she absent-mindedly filled four mugs from the kettle, scooping spoonfuls of sugar into each one.

'No sugar for me, thanks, Miss,' said Emmi hastily. 'Leave it,' she mouthed at the boys. 'She's got enough to worry about.'

Suddenly Miss Carter stopped stirring, the teaspoon in mid-air. Her head drooped so that her long hair fell forward over her face.

'Oh Robbie,' she whispered. 'What harm did you ever do to anyone?'

Emmi went over to Miss Carter and put an arm round her.

Jon bit into another chocolate digestive with a look of alarm and Aidan shuffled his feet.

Emmi handed Miss Carter a tissue from the box, and the teacher dabbed her eyes.

Aidan thought about their teacher at the protest. The festival banner hanging across the room reminded him of how she'd rallied the crowds against the fracking; the way she'd stood up to Lord Berryman in the museum meeting. She seemed like a different person now; it was as if all the fire had gone out of her.

'Do you need any help getting stuff ready for this afternoon, Miss?' said Emmi.

'Thank you,' Miss Carter said. 'But it's all under control for now.

'I've got the part of Boudicca this year.' She forced a smile. 'I get to dye my hair red. It doesn't come better than that.'

Her face dropped, and she started adding more sugar to the teacups. She looked like she was going to cry again, and Aidan saw Jon shove a third chocolate biscuit into his mouth.

Aidan felt Emmi nudge him with her elbow. She raised her eyebrows, gesturing with her head towards the window.

The rain had actually stopped, Aidan realised. A slice of sun was peeping through the clouds and lighting up the weapons on the table.

'Thanks for the biscuits and tea, Miss,' Emmi said. 'But we should be going now. If there's anything we can help with though, just send us a message. See you at the festival later!'

They pulled on their wellies at the door.

'There is one thing ... ' Miss Carter's voice faltered as she stood in the doorway. She cleared her throat. 'Maybe it's silly ... ' Then she shook her head. 'No. Don't worry.'

'Tell us!' Aidan chorused with the others.

'Well,' Miss Carter continued slowly. 'Well, when you do see Robbie, Emmi, could you put this on his bedside?'

She held out a small figure carved from wood. A hare. 'He's forever giving me cute little presents as you know and, well, it's something I made for him. A Celtic charm. A healing charm actually. For good luck. I wanted to do something, and didn't know what. Silly I know. But I always was a superstitious thing!'

'It's really lovely,' said Emmi softly, squeezing her teacher's hand. 'Thanks, Miss.' She put the hare into her pocket. 'I'll keep it safe with me until I see him.'

OOO

The trees closed in. They were getting really near to the clearing now. The only sounds were their breathing and their footfalls on the narrow woodland path.

At one point a message pinged through on Aidan's phone from Dad; he was held up in the city and wouldn't be back for the festival. But Aidan managed to push away his worries about the chariot race. Imagine they found something in the clearing! Imagine the news he might have for Dad when he came back!

They broke out into the space, the huddled circle of woods at its edges. Aidan saw the mound rising from its shadowy centre, and the ancient horse chestnut tree that grew on its top, its thick roots breaking the surface of the slope. The strange pocket of silence where no creature stirred. Its eerie blue shadows.

Now he was here again, Aidan felt a strange awe.

He remembered the cloaked woman he'd seen there. That same face in the glass of the museum case, with its grey-green eyes.

A shiver brushed the back of his neck.

He thought about that aerial shot the drone had captured. The dark gold circle marking out this clearing like the shining centre of a target. The torrential rain would have washed away all traces of it now, for sure. But this was the place. He was certain of it.

'Come on!' Aidan said to the others, scrambling up the incline.

Close up, the ancient horse chestnut tree looked more dead than alive. It loomed over them, a cage of great branches twisting over and round in a gnarled mesh.

There is something here, Aidan told himself. *There has to be.*

Anything seemed possible in this secret place of mysterious mist-blue shadows.

Emmi and Jon looked at him, bright-eyed, and the three of them crouched in a line, ready to search.

'Let's find that tomb,' he said.

15

ROOTS

Aidan sat down heavily at the bottom of the mound.

'This is not looking good,' said Jon, trying to rub the mud off his face and instead managing to smear it all over his forehead. 'Operation Tomb Boudicca is crash and burn.'

Aidan bit his lip. They'd been searching for the best part of an hour; an hour of digging and scraping and tugging, and still they'd found nothing.

'We can't give up that easily!' Emmi scolded, waving her trowel at them. 'We've got to search again; even more carefully this time.'

Jon puffed his cheeks and blew out a breath. 'OK.'

They began to walk over the mound again, faces creased with concentration, making a spiralling path that gradually moved upwards, being sure not to miss any sections; checking old ground and being certain to include unexplored segments.

Nothing ... Nothing ...

Nothing.

And then ...

Jon let out a shout from the other side of the mound, and Aidan almost tumbled down the slope in his rush to get there.

The three crowded round the spot.

When you looked really closely, there was definitely something different about this patch of ground. There was a brownish tinge to the mossy covering, as if the plants had been ripped up and then stamped back down again. The sparse grass stuck out in spiky, withered patches. In places the knotty tree roots that riddled the surface were ragged.

Aidan knelt down. Emmi and Jon crouched to the ground as well, and all three started prodding the earth with their fingers and the points of the trowels; pulling at the thick, stubborn roots ...

Tree roots like snakes.

For some reason, Robbie's words came into Aidan's head as he worked, and they reminded him of just that. The leathery strands seemed to move disconcertingly under his touch, as if they were alive, and curled round his fingers in a none-too-pleasant way. All in his imagination, of course.

He heaved at one of the roots, digging his heels into the slippery slope to get a better grip. There was a ripping and a snapping sound and he tumbled backwards in a damp shower of dislodged soil.

At first the ground had seemed solid, but after some stabbing and scooping, more soil began to crumble away – unexpectedly downwards, the sound of the pieces showering against a surface somewhere deep inside.

The three of them stared at each other, and then Aidan jabbed the trowel harder. Excitement growing, he began kicking hard at the patch, the others joining in.

All of a sudden the patch of ground in front of him caved inwards, clods of earth collapsing to leave a gaping hole.

A moist, cool smell wafted up.

'Woah.' Jon gazed in amazement. 'Operation Tomb Boudicca is ... is ... ' His words dried up, and he swallowed. 'Have we found it?' he asked.

Aidan peered into the gloomy space, heart hammering.

'Do you think this is it?' said Emmi in a thrilled whisper.

Aidan felt his breath catch as his eyes adjusted.

Because there, inside the hole, were steps.

Steps.

A narrow, stone stairway descending into shadow.

The three of them exchanged stunned glances, and then,

with only the slightest hesitation, Aidan started to go down into the dark, cool silence.

The steps quickly levelled out and they found a passageway, a narrow tunnel curving out of view.

Bones through the gaps ... More of Robbie's words echoed unnervingly round Aidan's mind ... *Trapped down there in the dark* ...

But they soon gave way to another internal voice, one it was impossible to keep quiet – his own:

We've found the entrance to Queen Boudicca's tomb!

16

UNDER CARRUS MOUND

Aidan took out his mobile to turn on the torch, noticing there was no signal.

'We're out of range down here,' whispered Jon.

Aidan turned on the light and their shadows stretched up the rutted walls of the tunnel, only wide enough for single file.

Recover her bones from the Roman foe ... The Carrus chant ran through Aidan's head as he led the way. It was kind of calming. *Hide the tomb where none dare go. Bury her bones. Bury her sword, In a stone-carved tomb, with a royal hoard.*

Royal hoard. Aidan's skin prickled. What *were* they going to find?

He thought about the gold bracelets showing Boudicca and her daughters in their chariot. They were only the beginning! There was that magnificent sword Jon had read about, the hare with the huge ruby eye engraved on its hilt.

If this tunnel *was* going to lead them into Boudicca's tomb, the find was bound to stop the fracking before it could start. The Enershale deal would fall through, Berryman would keep his horses, and he and Dad wouldn't have to leave Carrus and could continue looking after Centurion. The plan tingled deliciously through Aidan's mind.

'Looks dodgy up there.' Jon eyed the roof as they crept on, and Aidan now saw the cracks criss-crossing overhead. The closer he looked, the more the whole thing appeared to be held together by nothing more than the lattice of horse chestnut tree roots dangling like ragged nooses of rope. He swallowed, trying not to think about the tons of rock and soil right above their heads.

The only sounds were the echoes of their footsteps and their breathing.

Despite the risk, this place *felt* so right to Aidan. He half-expected the ghostly flames of the will-o'-the-wisps to appear ahead of him, or the sadly beautiful figures of Boudicca's daughters beckoning them forward.

He followed a curve in the passage, then drew to a sudden halt. Emmi and Jon bunched up behind him. 'Look at that!'

Ahead of them the passage gave way to a low doorway framed by pitted columns of rock, the beam of light from his phone lost in the space beyond. He exchanged glances with Emmi and Jon, then stooped to go inside.

Aidan found himself in a kind of small underground cave. He used the light to trace out the slab stone walls, and a low, rock and earth ceiling. He held his breath, illuminating and investigating the room. Emmi had pulled torches from her rucksack for her and Jon, and the three of them fanned out, searching along the floor, the walls, and every corner ...

A crushing feeling grew in Aidan's chest as he combed the whole area.

Emmi's voice was incredulous, echoing round the chamber. 'There's nothing here!'

'But ... ' Jon stuttered. 'But, there has to be!' His beam flitted over the floor and walls, more and more erratically.

Aidan rested his forehead against the cold, hard wall.

'It's just an old bunker or something.' Emmi's voice was thick with disappointment as she lowered her torch. 'Maybe from the war, who knows? It's nothing but a dead end.'

'But might someone have been in here?' said Jon desperately. 'They could have taken whatever was inside!'

'This isn't the tomb. It can't be!' Emmi swept a hand round the space. 'Does this look like the stone-carved tomb of a Celtic warrior queen to you? There's no engravings in the rocks at all!'

'Unless you count graffiti,' said Jon. 'Come and look at this.'

They gathered round Jon to examine something scratched into the stone wall; a patch of letters and numbers.

'*BP*,' read out Jon. 'And a date. From ten years ago. Huh!

'Even if this *was* the right place,' he said glumly, 'any treasures were cleared out long ago. This place isn't going to convince anyone; and especially not by seven o'clock this evening when the fracking starts!'

Aidan let out a shout of frustration.

Above him he heard a faint, but definite creaking, like the earth was shifting a little, and a drizzle of powdery soil was caught in his torch beam.

Jon gripped his arm. 'Keep your voice down, Aide!' he hissed. He jabbed a finger at the ceiling, and Aidan saw the cracks he was pointing at.

'I think we should go,' whispered Jon. 'Mission abort! There's no way that roof's stable. And I tell you, we do *not* want to be down here if that lot caves in.'

17

COLD LIGHT OF DAY

Aidan's stomach churned as they made their way back through the narrow passage. He climbed up the gloomy stairway and broke out into the weak sunlight. Jon and Emmi stood by him, blinking and panting.

Aidan leant against a tree trunk and closed his eyes. He hadn't got a clue what to do next.

And as if that wasn't bad enough, Berryman was still expecting to see Centurion pulling the chariot in that afternoon's re-enactment. Now what was going to happen?

As Aidan stood there, his phone came back online. An email from Mr Williams appeared in his inbox marked URGENT. It was copied to the long list of people in the anti-fracking group.

Emmi and Jon had the same message on their phones and all of them opened the email link.

BREAKING NEWS

They stared at each other in disbelief as they simultaneously scanned the story.

'It's not possible!' Emmi gasped.

'No way!' stuttered Jon.

An age-old question about where Queen Boudicca's final battle with the Romans took place may finally have been answered, with a startling new find in the Watling Street area of the Midlands.

'But that's miles away from Carrus!' protested Aidan.

'An arm bracelet has been unearthed,' Emmi read out loud as Aidan enlarged the image on his phone, *'bearing the royal symbol of Queen Boudicca ...'*

'But it's the same!' Jon interrupted as Aidan peered at the screen. 'It's the one Robbie sketched – the bracelet stolen from the museum!'

Emmi frowned as she continued to read.

'But this sensational artefact was just the beginning. In the same grave the skeletons of two girls were found ...'

'*What?*' said Aidan. His shoulders tensed.

'Preliminary tests indicate that the bones are likely to be first century,' went on Emmi, *'and several historians have proposed they could credibly be ...'*

She gazed up at the boys.

'Boudicca's daughters.'

Aidan swallowed. 'The bracelet and bones must have

been put in a fake spot by whoever stole them!'

'Yeah,' agreed Jon. 'Probably by the same person who ran Robbie down to shut him up.'

'The same person who doesn't want Queen Boudicca getting in the way of the fracking!' spat Emmi. She frowned. 'Someone from Enershale, I bet. Or a corrupt Westminster politician!'

'Special government forces,' suggested Jon darkly.

'But what proof do we have of any of this?' Emmi said. 'Robbie's the only one who can back us up.' She looked at the ground. 'And he's not going to be talking any time soon,' she murmured.

Aidan's thoughts churned. He had the niggling feeling that he was missing something. Something important.

'We should have gone to the police when I said,' muttered Jon.

'No point trying to lay blame on other people, Jonathan Clegg!' Emmi snapped back. 'I seem to remember it was *you* who said we shouldn't!'

'Jonathan!' Aidan stopped suddenly, grabbing Jon's arm and shaking it so his friend went wide-eyed in alarm. 'BP!'

'What?' Jon shrugged. 'I'm totally lost, Aide.'

'The graffiti in the chamber!' Aidan told him. 'Jon's short for Jonathan. What's *B* short for?' He appealed to

Emmi to cotton on.

She shook her head at him at first, but then turned it into a rapid nod.

'Bob!' she exclaimed.

'Robbie!' she and Aidan said together.

'BP is Robbie Pickersgill!' said Emmi. 'Everyone used to call him Bob when he was younger.'

'Robbie *did* find the bracelet down there!' said Aidan. 'The bones too, but he left them in peace; remember what he said?' He thought a moment to get Robbie's words exactly right. *'Got to leave those kind of bones where you find them ... wouldn't be right.'*

'Yes!' said Emmi. 'By *those kind of bones*, he meant human bones! Then someone with zero respect came and put them and the bracelet in a completely different place to fool everyone and ... oh!' Emmi suddenly covered her mouth with her hand. *'That's* why!' she said.

'Why the daughters appeared to us! Why *now*! Don't you see?' she gasped. 'It's because their bones were stolen! Their final resting place was disturbed!

'But Boudicca's body can't have been with them,' she added. 'Or *her* bones would have been planted at the fake place as well, to make the find as convincing as possible.'

'That's true,' said Jon. 'Her tomb must be somewhere else.'

'Maybe there'll be clues as to who the thief was.' Aidan scanned around the hole. 'A footprint or something.'

'Not much chance after all that rain,' said Jon doubtfully. 'But let's look anyway.'

They started to hunt around in the bushy undergrowth. After long minutes of searching, Emmi gave a shout and held something in the air. A spade.

'Well, that would explain how they got in,' said Aidan, examining it. 'This is the same make as the tools we use on Berryman's estate.'

'Doesn't mean much,' said Emmi. 'Anyone could have got hold of it.'

Aidan kicked the ground. 'So what now?'

The three of them stood in silence a while.

'We could check the drone video again,' Jon suggested doubtfully. 'In case we missed some clue about the hit-and-run driver. I mean, the thief and the driver have to be connected. That's if they're not the same person.'

'It's worth a try,' said Emmi.

'There *was* that red car, right?' Jon said. 'The one we saw before the ambulance arrived. If we can zoom in on it using some special software I've got ... who knows? We're really running out of time and options.'

'The laptop's at my house with the drone, remember,'

said Aidan, as they left the clearing.

'We can connect the computer to my mum and dad's big telly,' said Emmi.

'And I've the software to analyse the film back home,' said Jon.

Plans ran through Aidan's head as they made for the edge of the woods. He felt a small surge of hope.

'OK,' he said, as they reached a fork in the path where the trees petered out. 'I'll run back for the laptop. You go get the software, Jon. Meet at Emmi's as soon as we can.'

'Yes, Chief!' Jon gave him a small salute, then turned and headed off, Emmi close behind him.

'Be careful everyone!' Aidan heard her call, as he sprinted off in the other direction across a field.

OOO

After five minutes of hard running, Aidan arrived in the yard by his house, panting.

As he got to the door, he stopped, his heart further speeding up.

He thought he'd seen a movement in an upstairs landing window. Was Dad back after all? It couldn't be him – there was no sign of their car.

But when Aidan looked again, he realised that the little

top window was open a notch on its catch. *Just the curtain*, he told himself, *fluttering in a draught.*

He didn't know why he was so jumpy. Probably the thought that Berryman could turn up at any moment to check on Centurion, his prize chariot horse. He'd seen the Lord's red Porsche up by the mansion as he passed the driveway. Quite a few other cars were parked there as well, some with *Enershale* painted along the sides.

Aidan let himself in with his key and went into the hallway.

The house felt strangely empty. Knowing Dad was away just made things worse. Packing boxes were piled up against one wall, some already sealed with brown tape, the top ones with their flaps gaping open to put the last few things in.

The sleeve of Mum's coat brushed against Aidan as he turned to shut the front door; the coat he and Dad kept on the hook, and that neither of them could bring themselves to put away.

For a moment or two he thought that he detected a faint smell – perfume, flowery, like Mum used to wear.

Now he really was just freaking himself out. *Get a grip!*

He tiptoed upstairs. *Why are you creeping about*, he asked himself? Still, the house seemed eerily desolate, as if it sensed they were leaving, and had already decided not to be their home any more.

Aidan reached the landing and stopped, hand clutching the top banister.

The door to his mum's study was closed.

He frowned. He and Dad always kept that open. Shutting it ... well, it just didn't seem right. Mum's door was never closed.

Aidan went and pushed the door wide, standing a few moments to look inside.

He and Dad liked to see Mum's things whenever they went upstairs. Her computer on the desk with its yellow Post-it notes stuck round the screen; her bookshelves crammed with a rainbow of book spines. On a sunny day, the light spilled in over her favourite wicker chair where she'd sit to write; over the patchwork blanket Aidan used to tuck round her knees in those last weeks to stop her getting cold. Until that day ... he stared at the floor as he remembered ... until she had been too sick to write any more.

That last book she'd never finished.

Aidan swallowed and turned towards his bedroom.

Dad had shut Mum's door by accident in his hurry to leave for the city, Aidan told himself – that must be it.

But somehow it still didn't feel right.

The curtains in Aidan's room were drawn, but he didn't bother to open them; there was enough light to find what he needed. He knelt to rummage in the space at the back of his wardrobe, shifting the drone to one side and then lifting out Jon's laptop that was tucked behind it.

It all happened in a second.

There was a noise behind him, and as his head whipped round a figure loomed up. Someone wearing a balaclava mask.

There was no time to react. No time to try and make out who it was in the gloom. No time to even get to his feet.

Gloved hands clawed forward to take the laptop and instinctively Aidan hugged the computer to his chest, struggling to keep a grip as the intruder tried to wrench it off him.

'Get off!' Aidan staggered up, desperate to reach the door, but was pushed with such force that his back slammed against the wall. A sharp pain seared across his shoulders. His arms sagged but still he clung to the computer, his thoughts on overdrive.

The drone file. The only copy. They're after the file. Can't let them get it!

The intruder lurched, landing a kick in Aidan's chest and he stumbled back with a strangled breath, his grip loosening. A gloved fist came at him and the impact of it ricocheted off his jaw and he was thrown off balance, crashing against the chest of drawers, then falling, the laptop slipping ...

Aidan pulled up his arms to protect himself, but it was too late.

His head smacked the wood of the floorboards.

Then ...

Nothing.

18

EAGLE

'Aidan! *Aidan!*'

'Man down!'

Slowly, the room swam into focus. Sunlight through a gap in the curtains.

It hurt to blink. He couldn't see so well out of one eye, and there was the tinny taste of blood in his mouth.

'He's coming round, Jon! He's waking up. Oh, thank god!' Emmi's voice. 'But we should still ring an ambulance and – '

Aidan shot out a hand. 'Don't!' he said groggily. It hurt to speak, like his insides were all bruised. 'Don't – call – any – ambulance!'

He heaved himself up to sitting.

'The police – will get – involved.' He took a painful breath. 'Don't want that.'

'But we *have* to!' said Emmi shakily. 'Aidan – you've been attacked! You have to tell us what happened. When you didn't show up at mine, we came round here straight away. We were so worried. And now the laptop's gone, isn't it? We should *never* have left you to go off alone. I feel so bad! If only we'd stayed together!'

Aidan tried to clear his thoughts. He was in enough trouble with the police; did he really want to get them involved? 'We need to think this through first,' he wheezed.

'Did you see who it was?' asked Emmi, her voice still trembling.

Aidan shook his head. 'They were wearing a balaclava.'

'Was there *anything* about them you remember?' Emmi persisted. 'There has to be something. Their height? Their eye colour?'

'The room was too dark. They were fast and strong, that's pretty much all I know.'

'But what about forensics?' said Jon. He was pale as a ghost. 'If the police can find fingerprints ... '

'Whoever it was wore gloves,' Aidan told him. 'There won't be any.'

Jon suddenly clicked his fingers. 'The camera on the drone! It'll have the original file still stored on it!' He began to search the room, then stopped dead with a short gasp of dismay. He stooped down, lifting up the drone, which Aidan saw was even more mangled than before.

Its camera bracket empty.

'Dronie!' Jon wailed, trying in vain to fix a broken propeller back in place.

'Whoever it was really wanted to make sure they got rid of all possible evidence,' Emmi said grimly.

Jon paced nervously to the window. 'Somehow they know who we are now, guys!' he said in a scared whisper. 'There must be at least two of them, I reckon. One must have seen us with the drone that day, while the other was in the hit-and-run car. They realised the video footage could incriminate them, so one of them came to steal the laptop.'

'But why wait till now?' said Aidan. 'Doesn't make sense.'

'Dunno.' Jon edged back the curtain. 'But they could be watching us right this very minute.'

Aidan let Emmi help him to his feet. Whatever the reason, their one chance to find out who had hurt Robbie; their one chance to find out how all this was connected to the stolen bracelet – that chance was gone.

The three of them sat glumly on Aidan's bed in silence, each lost in their own thoughts.

'You've got a lovely black eye there, man,' said Jon at last, with a tight grin.

'Maybe we should call the police after all,' said Aidan.

'What's that?' Emmi leant forward suddenly, scooping

something from the floor and holding it up.

Aidan saw a bent pin, a badge of some kind.

An eagle with outstretched wings. A word underneath ...

'The intruder must have dropped it during the attack!' said Emmi.

... *ENERSHALE!*

'This *proves* who's behind this!' she told them angrily. 'And it all makes perfect sense!'

Jon looked at Aidan.

'Enershale wants the fracking to happen, no matter what!' continued Emmi. 'The drilling's worth millions to them.'

'It does seem to fit,' Jon said slowly.

'So when they found out Robbie's uncovered the bracelet – proof that Boudicca was right slap bang in their fracking zone – they had to do something about it.' Her voice trembled with emotion. 'Steal the bracelet, cover the theft up, and shut Robbie up.'

'Probably the only reason you're still alive now, Aidan,' said Jon, 'is because your dead body would have attracted too much suspicion.'

'Thanks a lot,' said Aidan.

Emmi waggled the badge in the air. 'We can take this straight to the police as proof!'

'Hang on! We won't get a conviction based on some

mangled badge,' Jon told her. 'Sorry, but we'll need way better evidence than that, Em.'

Emmi stopped pacing and stood, twisting her hands together.

'Right,' she said determinedly, forehead creased in thought. 'If it's evidence we need,' she said under her breath, her eyes narrowing, 'then evidence is what we'll get.'

A thought hit Aidan. In all the confusion, it had gone straight out of his head. *The chariot race! Berryman!*

'Centurion!' he cried. 'What time is it?'

Emmi checked her watch. 'Nearly three o'clock.'

'I've got to get to the stables!' Aidan was already making for his bedroom door. If Berryman got there before him and saw Centurion's injury ...

What was he going to say when he was asked why Centurion wasn't racing? He still had no plan. He'd been so carried away with the tomb and finding Robbie's attacker ...

'Aidan!' said Emmi. 'There are still two hours before the race starts. But maybe you shouldn't go to the festival at all after what you've been through. You could be concussed.'

'Yeah, your skull could be fractured,' Jon said helpfully. 'Anyway, nobody will expect you to race with that black eye, and with your dad away ... '

Aidan spun to a stop as Jon's words sunk in. Then he

laughed out loud. It hurt to grin, but he did it anyway.

Yes! It was the perfect get-out for Centurion! Take the attention away from the horse's injury and place it on himself!

'Jon-Boy, you're a genius!' he said. 'Thank you, attacker!' he hollered out loud, punching the air with his fist.

Emmi looked confused. He saw her exchange a worried glance with Jon.

'*The blow to the head*,' he saw Jon mouth back at her.

'I'm not crazy, guys!' Aidan told them. 'But think about it! Only Dad or I can handle Centurion, Berryman knows that. Even *he's* not stupid enough to risk having someone else do it and something going wrong in front of the whole village and all his important friends. He'll *have* to use Firefly instead!'

'She's a much more docile horse,' agreed Emmi, smiling. 'Either way, Berryman won't even bother going to look for Centurion. He'll be too busy finding someone else to drive the chariot, so his friends still have a chance to win their bets.'

'We need to go over to Berryman's house right now to tell him!' Aidan said. 'You two can back me up about how I got the black eye. We can get our story sorted on the way over there.'

'Good!' said Emmi. She gave Aidan a cunning look.

'Going over to His Lordship's house was just what I was thinking anyway.'

'Yeah?' said Aidan as the three of them headed downstairs.

'All those Enershale people are there,' Emmi told them. 'Any one of them could have left the party, slipped here to steal the laptop, then still been back in time for cigars and brandy! While we're in there, we're going to look for clues as to which one of them attacked you.'

Jon looked uncertain. 'How are we going to do that then?'

'Well I haven't worked that out yet,' said Emmi. 'But come on!'

They reached the front door and Aidan paused a moment, turning to his friends.

'From now on, we stay together, right? Whoever it is behind this, we know they're on to us. And we know what they're capable of.'

Jon nodded hard. Emmi linked arms with him and Aidan, her face determined.

Aidan pulled open the door and they stepped outside.

19

THE SECRET FILE

Aidan went up the gravel drive towards the manor house, past the parked Enershale cars. Berryman's Porsche was still there as well. So far so good.

He chewed the inside of his cheek, running through the story they'd agreed on.

After several suggestions, including ones from Jon about Aidan being stampeded by a herd of cows, or being hit by a low-flying duck, Emmi had convinced them to go for something as close to the truth as possible. He and Jon had been messing about wrestling in his bedroom. He'd stumbled backwards and hit his face on a chest of drawers. Been knocked out.

They climbed the steps to the columned front door.

The plan would work, he told himself.

It had to.

Aidan reached for the doorbell.

Then a horrible idea occurred to him.

Berryman. What he stood to gain from the Enershale deal. The money he must be getting paid for the fracking to be on his land; the expansion plans that were set to take over the horse paddocks.

But *attempted murder*? He wouldn't go that far, would he?

Nah! Aidan pushed the thought away and pressed the bell.

They seemed to be waiting there ages before the grand front door swung open.

The old housekeeper told them Lord Berryman was finishing lunch with his guests. When Emmi insisted dramatically that it was a matter of life and death, the woman sighed, glanced suspiciously at Aidan's black eye, and showed them into Berryman's office to wait.

'I could get used to this,' said Jon, settling himself in the plush leather swivel chair behind the vast oak desk then spinning himself around as fast as he could.

Emmi gazed at the huge Persian rug in the centre of the room. 'As if Berryman needs even *more* money from fracking,' she said, wrinkling her nose as she fingered the gold-plated pen in its marble holder. 'Look.' She pointed to a line of bags and briefcases under jackets on hooks. 'Must belong to Berryman's guests.'

Jon swept up the receiver of the expensive-looking antique telephone. 'No more excuses!' he barked, pretending to be some kind of American army general. 'I want *results*, d'ya hear?' He banged a fist on the polished wooden surface. 'And I want them *now*!'

He sat back in the chair, grinning, plonking his feet on the desk. 'I could *definitely* get used to this!'

'Stop messing about!' Emmi snapped. 'He could come in here any minute!' She darted behind the desk and opened a drawer.

'Em, what are you *doing*?' Aidan hissed, eyeing the door.

'I *told* you,' Emmi said, rifling through the papers filed inside. 'We need to look for clues as to who's behind all this. We know Berryman is doing deals with Enershale. Maybe there'll be a list of the employees working on his land, or something like that.'

She pulled out a folder and slapped it on the desk. Aidan saw the Enershale eagle emblem stamped on the front.

He watched Emmi open the cover and look through the papers inside.

'The manager of the project is called Mr Frank Kimley,' she said, running her finger down a page. 'There's a mention of a site foreman,' she said, waggling a sheet. 'Someone called Charles Pearson ... and a list of the management team: Gavin Lewisham, Jean-Paul LeMan, John Bellshore, Sundeep Shah, Edwina Timms, Verity McDougal ... '

She took a quick photo of the page with her phone as Jon came to peer over her shoulder. 'We'll be checking all these people out on Google, soon as we get a chance.'

She flicked through a few more papers. 'Nothing much else interesting here as far as I can tell.'

'Hang on – what's that?' said Jon, selecting a sheet. 'Says: *geological map of fracking area* ... Er, Emmi.' He looked over as she snapped open the clasp of one of the briefcases. 'Are you sure you should be doing that?'

'Course! This bag belongs to F. Kimley himself – see the name on the side?' Emmi pulled out a wodge of stapled papers and scanned a page.

Aidan saw *PRIVATE AND CONFIDENTIAL* printed across the top in red.

'Listen to *this*!' she hissed.

'*On successful completion of the first fracking operation,*' Emmi read quickly, '*in order to extend the scheme and maximise the quantities of extracted shale gas over the longer term, four million pounds is to be paid to the landowner of adjacent land ...* '

Aidan gaped at her. *Four million?*

' *... J. Berryman agrees to cooperate fully with any expansion of operations ...* '

'Emmi!' She stopped reading abruptly at the panic in Jon's voice.

He was staring at the door. Aidan saw the fancy silver handle rotate.

Quick as a flash, Emmi had gathered the papers and stuffed them back into the briefcase. She swung round, whipped the folder back in the drawer and slid it shut.

The door began to open.

Aidan saw that Jon still had the map in his hand. He desperately eyed the desk, but there just wasn't time to put it back in the drawer now. He dived to snatch the paper and stuffed it into his belt at the back of his jeans.

The door swung wide and Lord Berryman hurried in.

'Kids,' he said impatiently, with a fake smile on his boyish face. 'This is kind of a busy time for me.' He stopped talking, obviously just noticing Aidan's black eye.

'Been scrapping, have you?'

Aidan poured out the practised story in a bit of a daze, Emmi and Jon adding useful details where needed.

'Right,' said Berryman, when Aidan had finished. He pushed the fringe away from his face irritably, and the hair flopped back like a dirty blonde curtain. 'But won't your father be back in time to race Centurion?'

Aidan shook his head. 'There are complications with the new flat. Dad sent a message. He won't be back until this evening.'

'I see.' He stared hard at Aidan, his mouth set into a tight line; Aidan shifted uncomfortably, hoping the paper in his belt wouldn't rustle and give him away.

'But you've won the race the last three years on the trot!' Berryman said with a childish whine to his voice. 'All my guests have bet on us to win. I told them it was a certainty.'

Aidan could almost see the calculations going on in Berryman's mind: *Can I get away with forcing a boy with a black eye to race?*

'Firefly has already practised pulling the chariot,' Emmi said quickly, 'and she was running really well.'

'Even without Centurion,' Jon put in, 'your horse will still win the race, Lord Berryman, sir. There's ... er, high-tech suspension, increased tyre traction ... um, state-of-the-art precision engineering.' He beamed broadly. 'Those high-and-mighty Roman generals won't stand a chance!'

He saw Berryman's eyes narrow. He paced the room so that Aidan had to shift position to keep the paper hidden.

'Well!' Berryman snapped at last. He sat down in his chair with a creak of leather. 'It can't be helped, I suppose.'

A wave of relief flooded over Aidan. His legs went a bit trembly with the sensation. *Centurion is safe!* They'd bought some time. For now, he was *safe*. He wanted to laugh out loud, but managed to control himself.

Berryman drummed his fingers on the desk. 'I'll have to draft in another stable hand to race,' he said.

He looked sharply at Aidan. 'But you hitch up that mare!' he said sharply. 'And get the chariot to the starting line. That will still be *your* responsibility, young man!'

Firefly. Aidan felt a flush of anger as he nodded. Lord Berryman couldn't even be bothered to use the horse's name when he spoke about her!

But that was nothing to the anger that was now building up in him as what Emmi had read sunk in. *'Four million pounds ... landowner ... Lord J. Berryman ... expansion of operations ...'*

Berryman was going to make way more money from the fracking operations than he'd been letting on. And that secret document proved this first drilling was only the beginning. Once that was up and running, the way was open for more and more fracking. Who knew where that would end up?

He swallowed. It had, after all, been a *red* car speeding from Robbie's accident.

Berryman was now well and truly *Suspect Number One.*

He studied the man's face, but he wasn't letting anything slip. Sure, Aidan could see Berryman was totally irritated about Centurion not racing, but how he managed to stand there right in front of them and be so false, with all the other stuff going on, it was just plain sinister.

Was it Berryman himself who had attacked Aidan in his house?

Knowing His Lordship, he had probably got someone else to do the dirty work, an accomplice probably. Which one of them had taken the bracelet and started the museum fire?

'Thanks Lord Berryman,' Aidan mumbled. He started to edge slowly backwards. 'We'd better be going now. Get ready for the festival.'

'Yes,' said Emmi stiffly, as she and Jon also made for the door. 'I need to talk to my parents. Find out how *Robbie* is,' she said, putting slightly too much emphasis on the name. Aidan could see she was struggling to hold it together.

As Aidan closed the door, he saw Berryman watching him from behind the desk, their eyes locking a moment; an unreadable expression on the man's face.

OOO

'Woah!' Jon sank back against a brick post. They were well down the drive and out of sight of the manor house. He blew out his cheeks, 'That was extreme!'

Aidan sat heavily on a patch of lawn, his heart still thudding.

Carried on the breeze was the sound of a brass band warming up; the jolly thump of a bass drum. The smell of barbecuing meat drifted upon the air; the Iceni Festival was gearing up to start. Aidan could make out the white marquees set up in one of the big fields; the multicoloured bunting strung along the fence posts.

'He seemed to believe the black eye story,' Emmi said uncertainly. 'But did you see the looks he was giving you, Aidan? It was obvious that he was hiding something. Oh, if *only* we could have got a photo of that document!' she said in frustration.

'We should check those names out though,' said Aidan. 'What were they again? Gavin Lewisham, Edwina Timms and that. Who knows who else is involved on the Enershale side?'

'We've got to be even more super careful from now on – you realise that, don't you?' said Emmi. 'If Berryman finds out we know all about the Enershale deal ... '

'It really has to be him behind all this, doesn't it?' said Jon. 'Oh man!'

'He'll pay for what he did to Robbie,' Emmi said quietly. She fingered her hair in agitation. 'But we have to stay one step ahead of him. Keep our heads. Work out how to get that evidence.'

Aidan nodded, but doubt gnawed at him. *Berryman?* Capable of trying to *kill* someone? The man was a lot of things, but a *murderer*? Everything pointed to James Berryman, but it still seemed unbelievable.

'What if he realises something's gone from his folder?' Aidan cast a glance in the direction of the house, and then pulled out the crumpled paper.

'Maybe it's not so important,' said Emmi. 'We've got to hope he won't miss it.'

They sat in a huddle as Aidan unfolded the sheet and smoothed it out. The thin map covered their laps when it was fully open.

'That's Carrus marked on there,' said Jon, tapping the place with a finger. The excitement grew in his voice as he continued to study the drawing. He let out a low whistle. 'It's got all the data about the exact fracking schedule for this evening!

'See that?' Jon pointed at a thick red line, with red asterisks marked at intervals along it. 'It's the horizontal shaft that's already been excavated through the shale rock. A thousand metres below the ground. That's deep!

'And the asterisks ... they tell us where each fracking event is set to take place along the shaft. You know – where they will blast the rock to get the gas out.

'Let's see, a total of ... ' he counted quickly. 'Six blasts, each fifteen minutes apart.'

'And the first blast ... ' said Emmi, peering at the tiny number along the line. 'At 7 p.m. this evening. Right when the festival celebrations are in full swing.'

Seven o' clock tonight. Aidan's stomach did a somersault.

Emmi checked her watch. 'That's three hours from now! Berryman will be at the festival. We can watch him. Check who he talks to. See if we can get any leads on who he worked with to break into the tomb of Boudicca's daughters.'

'That's not good.' Aidan saw Jon was frowning, peering closer at the map. 'We'd better get some of those leads fast, guys,' he said.

'What do you mean?' asked Emmi.

'Blast number six.' Jon's fingertip came to rest on the final red asterisk along the fracking tunnel.

'It's set to go off right under Carrus Woods.'

20

CHARIOT RACE

'But the blasts will be too deep to affect the chamber, surely?' Emmi tapped the map. 'You said the fracking happens at 1,000 metres.'

'You saw the cracks in the ceiling, though,' said Jon. 'Yes, the blasts are deep, but we know they can trigger earth tremors. If that roof comes down, there'll be no way to prove that was the tomb of Boudicca's daughters.'

Aidan hastily folded the map back up. 'Berryman could go looking for this any time, and work out it must be us who took it.'

'Well there's no way we can return it!' said Emmi. 'It's all crumpled anyway. Best to just hide it somewhere for the time being.'

Jon nodded, taking it and cramming it into his pocket.

By now the brass band music had got louder and more tuneful; the wafting food smells stronger. Aidan detected burgers and frying onions. There were the sounds of cars parking and distant chatter. Hooves clattered along the lane and he heard the slightly rickety trundle of wooden wheels on tarmac. Then the first of the homemade chariots came into view, making its way to the race field.

'We've still to get Firefly to the starting line,' Aidan said. 'We'd better get moving.'

'And change into our Iceni costumes,' said Emmi, getting to her feet. 'We need to act normal; get close to Berryman. Watch who he's talking to, that kind of thing.'

The three made it to the shed where they'd stored the chariot, heaving it out on its two high wooden wheels, then quickly got to work, leading Firefly over and hitching her up.

Aidan felt a lump in his throat as he looked at Robbie's paintings along the chariot's side: Boudicca and her daughters in the chariot. The battle scenes. As they got into their costumes, he thought about Robbie's cryptic comment about having a 'best treasure'.

He had meant the bracelet – Aidan knew that now. He pulled at the bottom of his tunic. If only he'd asked Robbie more questions at the time and found out what he'd meant. If he had, Emmi's cousin might be here with them now, and not lying in a hospital bed.

Emmi linked her arm through his. 'Ready?' she said.

She was wearing a long woollen skirt, a dark green tunic, and had a blue spiral painted on each cheek. '*Recover her bones from the Roman foe!*'

'*Hide the tomb where none dare go!*' shot back Jon, and Aidan smiled a little as the three of them climbed up on to the chariot and he clicked Firefly into a gentle trot.

They made their way past the stalls and the milling crowds to the start line, where they'd meet up with Berryman's new rider. Other chariots joined them on the strip of field marked out with little flags, and the crowds on either side got thicker. Rival hare flags and eagle flags flapped from fence posts.

Pretty much everyone had dressed up for the occasion, either as Romans or Iceni Celts. Faces were painted with blue woad spirals and zigzags. People wore woollen tunics and trousers in shades of brown and green. Bare-chested men with spiked-up hair grinned and mock-wrestled each other.

People seemed determined to enjoy themselves, despite the fracking threat. Or had most of them just given up and accepted it was going to happen, no matter what?

Roman helmets bobbed about and standards were being carried, their eagle symbols glinting in the afternoon sunlight.

They passed a skipping game. *'Eternal sleep, forever in youth,'* young children chanted as they jumped the long rope. *'Guarded by leverets, Valour and Truth!'*

Aidan caught a glimpse of Miss Carter. She made a striking Boudicca, with her flowing hair dyed red. Bold, blue patterns were painted round her eyes and swirled up her bare arms like tattoos.

'Can you see Berryman?' said Emmi, as they neared the starting line.

Aidan scanned the teeming crowds on tiptoe.

'There!' said Jon. 'By the trophy table. I don't recognise the people he's with.'

'Let's get nearer,' said Emmi. 'See if we can go round the back of them and listen in on what they're saying!'

They jumped down from the chariot, and Berryman's replacement driver swung himself up and took the reins.

There was the usual party atmosphere of the festival, but also something more – Aidan felt it now as they made their way through the crowds – an underlying tension. People seemed more fired up than usual. He now saw anti-fracking placards, in amongst the Roman standards and leaping-hare banners.

Aidan noticed the weapons being carried around him as well. The daggers in leather belts; the long wooden bows and quivers of arrows on people's backs. The short, stabbing swords of the Romans, and their realistic, lethal-looking spears.

A horn was blown; long, wailing blasts, and Celts gathered on the site for the battle re-enactment in the adjacent field. Some held oval, hide-covered shields decorated with leaping hares that seemed to come alive as they were moved about. Weapons swiped the air, interlocking Celtic patterns glinting on their hilts.

Aidan couldn't help pausing to watch. Every year, it was always an awesome spectacle: the re-enactment of that last battle.

The heavily outnumbered Romans pressed into a tight formation opposite the Iceni, their bright red and gold shields curved round them like armour plating.

The Ancient Britons began beating their swords against their shields, a steady thudding, getting louder all the time. They began goading the enemy, shouting insults, casting fierce glares, as the beating din increased further and they prepared to charge.

A yell went up. The mock Iceni-Roman battle began.

The Roman soldiers shuffled forward, keeping rigidly in rank as they faced the teeming stream of Celts.

A shower of arrows with harmless plastic ends fell on

to the Roman defences. Iceni let out theatrical, blood-curdling cries and staggered backwards as authentic-looking javelins struck them with their foam tips. There was the clashing of blunt-edged swords, as people fought, hand to hand. Grins as fallen fighters were helped up and carried on fighting.

'Come on!' Emmi urged. 'Lord Berryman's just over there.'

They neared where he was sitting.

On the battlefield, the fighting seemed to grow in intensity. There were fewer smiles from the participants, Aidan noticed. The wild, savage shouts of the blue-painted Celts were deafening.

The Iceni drew back their bows, then let off another volley of arrows. A Roman reeled in realistic agony as he lost grip on his shield and a sword was plunged through him.

Aidan was suddenly uncomfortable with the whole idea of what he was watching. The re-enactment was no longer a bit of traditional theatre. What was this festival about anyway? A celebration of people getting killed?

Course not. Aidan knew that. But it all seemed wrong, like it was making a game out of a terrible event.

In the adjacent field, there was the crack of a pistol, and the chariot race started, heightening the feeling of chaos. As the chariots gathered speed, Aidan glanced at the galloping Firefly. The blurred number plate of their chariot, *AD61*, flew past.

The commotion of yells and chanting got louder. Drumbeats reverberated through the earth; screams cut the air. The throb of noise hurt his ears. Hostile faces were caught in the firelight of torches burning at the field's perimeter.

Aidan began to feel strange.

Pins and needles had started in his left fingertips. He clenched and released his fist to try and shake it off, but slowly the uncomfortable sensation was spreading, a numbness in his whole hand and then along the wrist towards his elbow. He flexed his knuckles, but the more he tried to ignore it, the worse it seemed to get, until the length of his arm was tingling. A gnawing panic started. His heartbeat quickened.

His vision went blurry. Strange shadows flitted over the scene. The thud of galloping hooves seemed to pound through him.

Aidan blinked. His head swam. He didn't feel at all well.

The numbness had started on the other side now too, spreading quickly along each side of his body and down his legs; a frightening, fizzing sensation, as if the blood supply had been cut off; as if tiny dots of electric charge were covering his skin.

His vision became really fuzzy. The landscape was changing in front of his eyes, features shifting and distorting.

What's happening?

Aidan reached out a hand to steady himself, but still the scene reshaped itself, like a set change at the theatre when, from behind a gauze, whole towns are lifted away in one sweep; whole forests are dropped into place where there were none before.

Familiar buildings went hazy and dissolved. The profile of the hill was still there, but there were way more trees now, growing densely on every side of the fields. And the fields themselves were marshy-looking, peppered with reeds and shimmering pools of water. The lake had shrunk and its sides got much steeper, so that it was now more like a deep pond or a boggy pit. On its surface, Aidan caught the occasional glimpse of a faint blue flame, flickering and shifting; appearing and vanishing.

His mouth went dry.

Rising up in front of him was a quite different battle scene.

Romans. Celts. But the arrows Aidan saw being drawn back from bows now had razor tips. The slashing sword edges were lethally sharp.

The drumbeats, the screams, the jarring bellowing of horns, all seemed to merge into one mass of sound.

His throat constricted.

People continued to fall on both sides of the battle, but of the ones on the ground, none of them were getting up any more.

At the boundaries of his sight were arcs of red blood as blades stabbed and slashed.

Aidan tried to take a step back, but couldn't. It was as if he was trapped in a kind of dream, unable to move his feet, only watch in horror.

The Romans continued their relentless tactic, keeping their nerve and their tight groupings. Even from this distance, it was easy for Aidan to see the success of their methods. There was a kind of bottleneck of fighting so that, even though there were way more Celts, only a limited number of them could get at the Romans at any one time. Channelled into the narrower strip of land between the trees, the Iceni fighters were being relentlessly picked off one by one.

Queen Boudicca's tribe was systematically being slaughtered.

A shout went up from behind him. Aidan saw Romans on horses weave out between the trees and pour forward.

He was right in their line of approach; they were coming straight at him, but still he couldn't move. He saw their swords pointed; the horses' misty breaths coming in bursts ... he could make out the colour of their eyes; their stares going through him and beyond to their targets as they accelerated forward ...

Aidan's mouth gaped as the charging horses were upon him. He felt his whole body tense, his back arch with a raw, bone cold as the spectres went right through and past him ...

He stood there, numb with the shock of it. On the battlefield he saw the sea of red uniforms swell, the mounted Romans reach the Celts. He saw the remaining Britons begin to fall back and retreat; those left trapped in the field abandoned to their deaths.

A shout went up – loud enough to carry over the noise of the fight.

Aidan gaped.

From behind Iceni ranks thundered a chariot pulled by two horses. Their hooves tore up the waterlogged soil as they pounded forward; their manes streamed back in the wind.

There was a woman at the reins, holding them high.

Either side of her was a tall girl: one with her cloak edged in fur, the other with her auburn hair braided in one great plait.

Aidan shuddered with recognition.

Boudicca's daughters.

And without the faintest doubt, he knew who was driving that chariot.

It was *Queen Boudicca.*

Was it her desperate bid to help the trapped tribesmen? One last act of defiance?

It was impossible to know for sure.

The wheels were a blur of movement. Boudicca raised a whip, then cracked it down, spurring the horses to go even faster ...

Out of nowhere, a Roman spear plunged towards the chariot.

One of the horses reared, in a stomach-turning spray of blood, letting out what was more a shriek than a whinny.

Aidan clenched his teeth. He saw the chariot swerve, tilt, the three occupants thrown violently to one side. The axle broke, and a wheel careered away. There was the sound of splintering wood. Sparks flew up as metal twisted and scraped against metal.

He saw the two horses slam the ground, sliding to a stop amidst the wrecked chariot.

Aidan held his breath. He saw the mother and daughters, lying still. There were dark patches of blood on their clothes.

Boudicca's head lifted slightly. He saw an arm move, then a leg, and she began to drag herself towards her daughters.

Aidan heard feet pound in time. A group of Romans had separated off from the others and were heading in their direction. A gold-black Roman banner seemed to fill the sky; an eagle with its wings outstretched, talons out.

Still Boudicca pulled herself forward. One of the daughters turned her face towards her mother; the other was trying to get up, but couldn't.

Aidan found himself right beside the three of them, transported there – he had no idea how. He could see Boudicca's face clearly, the face he had first seen between the branches in the clearing; the same face he'd seen reflected in the glass of the museum case.

The group of soldiers got closer.

Boudicca wrenched her sword from its scabbard with a cry, clutching it with bleeding hands. Aidan saw a leaping hare engraved in intricate swirls. He saw a ruby on the sword's hilt flash like an angry red eye.

He heard Boudicca call to her daughters. He could hear the desperation in her voice; the angry fear. But he was still powerless to do anything, only stand and watch.

Boudicca had reached her daughters and she was gripping them, speaking to them in a low and urgent voice, in a language he didn't understand.

And then, in the next second, the girls were being dragged to their feet by the soldiers, and Boudicca was crying out as they were wrenched away from her, calling to them in that ancient, forgotten Iceni dialect; repeating the same words over and over ...

In that moment, Aidan heard the words clearly. And as they came to him through the air, in that tiny moment of time before the words faded, somehow he understood that forgotten language.

'Truth!

'Valour!'

Boudicca was calling out their names.

Her daughters' names.

The scene began to shift and fade.

Aidan saw the girls pulled towards the deep marshy pond with its thin wisps of flame, but the vision was accelerating away from him in a blur of blue light until ...

A wave of sound broke round Aidan, as if he had suddenly surfaced from deep water. The upbeat pomp of a brass band with its sliding trombone notes. Laughter. The clank of blunt swords clashing against one another.

Blinking, gasping, Aidan watched grinning Roman soldiers help up Iceni and shake hands, or give each other bear hugs. The triangular bunting strung out along the fence posts flapped like waving hands.

The scene of the festival materialised once again.

Everything exactly as it had been.

21

VALOUR AND TRUTH

'What is it, Aidan?' Emmi's voice. 'What happened?'

'Did you see them?' he panted. His hands were still trembling like crazy. 'Did you see the battle?'

Jon nodded his head, glancing worriedly at Emmi. 'Er, yeah, Aide,' he said uncertainly. 'The re-enactment. We all saw it.'

'Not *that* one!' Aidan said. 'The real battle! Boudicca and her daughters!'

Aidan let Emmi and Jon help him round the side of a marquee, and they sat him on a patch of grass as he struggled to get his breath back.

'Maybe it's the knock to the head he got this morning,' Aidan heard Jon tell Emmi behind his hand. 'Delayed concussion.'

'We did see the horses in the race acting all weird,' said Emmi. 'Firefly went crazy! She was in the lead, but she stopped suddenly before the end and refused to cross the finish line. The driver was nearly thrown off. She would have won too. Berryman is furious!'

On the other side of the tent, Aidan could see the final part of the re-enactment being played out. Queen Boudicca, a.k.a. Miss Carter, being transported on a stretcher held up by grief-stricken Iceni, a solemn convoy to lay her in an imitation tomb of grey painted polystyrene.

The procession was walking in time to a sombre drumbeat.

'You look terrible, Aidan,' said Jon. 'I thought you were going to faint or something.'

'Tell us exactly what happened!' Emmi cried. 'You saw Boudicca's daughters again?'

Aidan nodded slowly. His head throbbed. How could he put into words what he'd witnessed? The killing. The horrible chariot accident. The girls taken to be killed. His chest twisted as he thought of it.

Emmi and Jon stared at him in amazement as he told them everything.

'Oh Aidan,' said Emmi, as she and Jon helped him to his feet. Her face was pale.

'It happened ... ' Aidan pointed as he located the place, '... right over there. Where the lake is now, only it was much smaller and deeper back then – more like a pit.'

'That would explain how we found one of the arm bracelets there,' Emmi said thoughtfully. She looked over at the lake. 'Sacrificial pits,' she murmured. She looked back at the boys. 'Remember, we read about those when we were researching the will-o'-the-wisps? They believed the flames were magic.

'Maybe the Romans ... ' Emmi winced. 'Maybe they sacrificed the daughters to give thanks to their gods for winning the battle. And if that's where they were killed, that could explain why their ghosts came to haunt that place when their bones were disturbed.'

Emmi swallowed. 'What I think is that at some time after the battle – maybe years later, who knows – surviving members of the Iceni tribe collected the bones of the daughters from the pit; maybe Boudicca's body was there as well. They gave them all a proper burial, in secret. They wouldn't have wanted the Romans to find out and destroy the graves.'

Aidan was still trying to get his head straight. The vision was telling him more – he just knew it. He racked his brains about what he was missing, but his sore eye throbbed so much he could hardly think. He forced himself to visualise the scene again: the battle, the overturned chariot, Boudicca crawling towards her daughters. Her tormented face as she cried out to them.

'But we know from the legend that the queen was buried alone,' frowned Emmi. *'Lay her to rest in a tomb of her own.'*

Aidan's confusion suddenly collapsed into something else: a stabbing sense of excitement.

Emmi's words came back to him; what she'd said about Boudicca's daughters: *Nobody knows what they were called.*

Aidan got up so fast that he nearly knocked Jon over. An elated panic spun through him. The answer had been staring them in the face all along! 'How long until the fracking starts?'

Jon fumbled to check his phone. 'An hour and ten minutes until the first blast ... but what about Berryman?' he said with a confused expression. 'I thought we were going to spy on him and ... '

'There's no time!'

Aidan's body jumped with an excited kind of electricity. That was it! That had to be it! He couldn't help give a wild little laugh. 'We need to get back to the clearing. *Now!* Go back down into the chamber Robbie found!'

'But it's a danger zone, Aide, man,' Jon protested. 'And there's nothing there. It's cleaned out. You saw the place.'

'Come on!' said Aidan. 'I'll explain as we go.'

Aidan's mind was in overdrive as they rushed full pelt towards Carrus Woods, and he gave his friends a tumbling explanation as they ran.

Guarded by leverets, Valour and Truth.

Leverets were young hares. Boudicca's young hares.

Her daughters!

All along, Aidan realised, the Carrus chant – passed down generation after generation – held the clue to everything.

Boudicca was buried *in a secret chamber of her own*, and that chamber was guarded by her own daughters. That meant that ...

'Boudicca's tomb has to be right next to her daughters' tomb!' exclaimed Emmi. She cast Aidan a grin and her eyes sparked. 'Oh my God! That makes total sense. I read once about how some tombs had secret chambers. The front part was used as a decoy, so if it was found it would be thought that was all there was. But the main part was hidden right behind!'

Somewhere in the background, Aidan was vaguely aware of a car in the lane.

'Boudicca's tomb must be somewhere in the underground complex!' Emmi declared. 'We just need to get back into the daughters' tomb and find the way into it.'

'The walls seemed pretty solid when we were last down there though,' Jon protested. 'Just rock and earth.'

'We need to check more carefully,' Aidan told him.

'Especially the wall right opposite the entrance, I reckon. We'll probably need to smash our way through.'

'That might take some serious hardware,' said Jon.

'Dad's work shed by the stables!' shot Aidan. 'We can grab some tools from there on our way past.'

They skidded to a stop in the yard and dashed inside the building.

'This looks good.' Aidan heaved a mallet from its hook and dropped it in a holdall. He rummaged around for other suitable equipment.

'This too,' said Emmi, grabbing a beefy claw hammer and shoving it in the bag.

She whirled round to face the boys suddenly. 'Imagine!' she told them breathlessly. 'Imagine being the first to go into Boudicca's tomb since she was buried there! Imagine what we'd find ... '

Jon added a crowbar and big torch to the bag. 'Yes, but let's not forget about the six fracking explosions,' he said worriedly. He got out his phone. 'The first will be at 7 p.m.,' he muttered. 'Then the others at fifteen-minute intervals after that.

'I'm setting a ten-second countdown for each. I want some warning before those things go off!'

Aidan pulled the bag up on to his shoulders and they

ran across the yard in the direction of the woods.

'And if we're still down there,' called out Emmi, 'when the last one hits?'

The question hung in the air, unanswered. Because at that moment Berryman's red Porsche slammed to a halt in the yard right in front of them, forcing them to stop. The door swung open and he jumped out.

'I knew we should have used Centurion to pull the chariot!' His cheeks were flushed as he strode towards them. Aidan smelled alcohol on his breath. 'You told me the other horse was a sure winner!' he told them. 'My friends all lost their bets!'

Before anyone could reply, Berryman was storming into the stables, Aidan following in panic.

The man came to a halt in front of Centurion's stall. His eyes bulged a little as he took in the scene. Centurion's bandaged leg; the bag of medication with Ann's surgery name stamped on it.

Then he spoke, spitting out each word like it was a bullet; his voice dangerously low.

'What – is – going – on – here?'

Centurion tossed his head, his hooves clattering the floor.

'He got an injury and you didn't tell me?' said Berryman coldly. 'You've been having him treated behind my back?'

'Dad's paying for it!' said Aidan defiantly. 'It isn't costing you anything!'

Berryman turned on him. 'You were lying to me, Aidan. All that rubbish about the black eye and not being able to race; it was all a story! Did you tell your dad to keep away too? He was obviously in on the whole thing!'

'No!' Aidan shouted. 'Dad had nothing to do with it! Anyway, you can't sack him twice!'

'I haven't sacked your dad, Aidan,' Berryman's mouth was a tight line. 'I have to let him go. With a more-than-fair redundancy package, I might add. Once the last horses are gone, I won't need ... '

'We have to leave because of you!'

'Calm down, Aidan!' he heard Emmi hiss from beside him. 'You'll only make things worse.'

But Aidan couldn't calm down. A wave of emotions was pressing down on him, threatening to swallow him up; all the feelings that he'd had to keep bottled up inside him all these weeks began spilling out.

'You would have had him put down!' Aidan was yelling now. Why was Berryman so bothered about Centurion anyway, with all the other things he was involved in? He must be some kind of monster. 'You'd have done the same as you did to Velvet Dancer when she went lame!'

'Centurion is *my* horse, Aidan!' Berryman's thin face was flushed with anger. 'It's my right to do as I choose. How dare you try and tell me what to do with my own horse!'

'Please, Lord Berryman,' Emmi came forward with her arms in a pacifying gesture. 'We all just need to stay calm, and let Aidan explain ... '

'Old Lord Berryman would have been ashamed of what you're doing!'

There. The words were out. Aidan felt his heart thump with fright, but he couldn't take them back now, and he hadn't finished saying what he was burning to say. 'Your dad would never have signed his land over to fracking just to make a load of money. He would never have got rid of the horses the way you're doing!'

He had to bite his tongue to stop himself saying more, about Robbie, the attack at his house ... he knew he'd already said way too much. 'Old Lord Berryman knew what Centurion meant to my mum,' he finished in a mumble.

Berryman stood there, stock still, staring at Aidan, as if he was seeing him for the very first time. For once in his life, he seemed at a loss for words.

Then his face took on a hard look. He snapped the cover off his phone. 'I'm calling the vet right now. And it won't be your precious vet I'll be calling, I can tell you that for nothing!'

Berryman turned away to dial.

'No!' said Emmi. 'Please, Lord Berryman!'

But he ignored her. 'Yes, Lord Berryman calling. I have an injured horse. I'd like you to come over – immediately if you can. Yes. It's very urgent.'

Aidan felt tears of anger prick his eyes. He had the sudden need to talk to Dad, to tell him everything that had happened, to get his help. But what was he going to say to him? He couldn't get back from the city now in time, even if he wanted to. And Berryman wasn't going to listen to reason, that was obvious.

Aidan knew one thing. He kicked the ground. There was no way he was going to let anything happen to Mum's favourite horse. A desperate plan took shape inside his head.

If Dad wasn't here to defend Centurion, Aidan was going to have to take matters into his own hands.

'The vet's coming.' Berryman couldn't look Aidan in the eye. 'I'm going to meet him in the lane,' he said shortly. He strode off towards the gate.

'He won't get away with it!' Aidan told Emmi and Jon through clenched teeth. 'Any of it!'

They were going to prove what was going on. Somehow they were going to uncover the truth.

And the only way to the truth now, was to find Boudicca's tomb.

Aidan took a length of rope and unbolted the wooden door to Centurion's stall.

The horse came towards him with an unsettled neigh, ears flat back, and Aidan stroked the animal's nose. 'I'll keep you safe,' he whispered fiercely.

Centurion gave a soft snort, nuzzling against Aidan's palm.

'Er, what are you planning, Aide?' said Jon, biting his nails.

Emmi said nothing. Instead she quickly went to where Centurion's halter was hanging from its hook, and lifted it down. With a nod at Aidan, she helped him to fasten it on to the horse's head, pulling the straps firmly in place.

'But isn't this *stealing*?' Jon warned. His eyes were wide. 'Centurion is still Berryman's horse ... ' His voice trailed off. 'How can I help?'

He would need to add stealing to his growing list of criminal activities, thought Aidan, along with arson and whatever else.

He attached a rope to the halter, looping it through the metal ring, and gave an urgent tug on the rope, leading Centurion out into the yard, Emmi and Jon following with the holdall of tools. The big horse's hooves skittered on the stone flags as he followed Aidan in the direction of Carrus Woods. The animal tossed his head, suddenly more alert, seeming to relish being out in the open again for the first time since his accident. Aidan was relieved to see there were no signs of a limp.

'Let's make it fast,' said Jon. 'The first fracking is in ... ' he checked the time on his mobile, '*twenty-five minutes*' time!'

Aidan made a clicking sound to Centurion and the four of them hurried for the trees.

Part 3

22

GUARDED BY LEVERETS

I won't let anything happen to Centurion, Aidan repeated to himself as they went.

All he knew was that he was going to hide the horse; keep him safe, somewhere near the clearing. He had to buy time until Dad got back and could try and sort things out. They reached the edge of the field, and headed into the ancient woodland. Emmi went first, then Jon, with Aidan leading Centurion at the back.

The trees closed round them, a sanctuary of branches and leaves. Sunlight came in beams through the canopy, moving in flitting patches on bark and heather.

Emmi called instructions as they made a hurried plan. 'We should tap along the walls of the chamber and listen for a sound that the face might be hollow ... Or look for marks that might show us where the hidden doorway is. There must be something we missed the first time.'

On they went, winding between the thickening trees.

Aidan tugged at the rope, and Centurion gave a rumbling snort of complaint; then continued his steady pace. There was no way to rush the horse more than he was already.

At one point they heard the distinct sound of a car engine, muffled by the trees, but uncomfortably close.

'Berryman, do you think?' asked Jon.

It had to be, Aidan reckoned, searching for them using one of the tracks at the wood edges. If Berryman stayed in his car, he wouldn't be able to follow them this far. But if he decided to continue on foot ...

'Come on!' Aidan hissed. 'We need to go further in.'

They got deeper into the woods, walking in silence. Even Emmi had stopped her nervous chatter.

Niggling doubts were never far away. What if they couldn't find the second chamber in time? thought Aidan. *Fracking Blast Number Six.* What might that do to those widening cracks in the rocks?

From behind, leaves rustled and twigs cracked, and Aidan started to get the uncomfortable feeling that someone was watching from the dense thickets and their steel-blue shadows. But when he peered nervously back the way they'd come, he couldn't see anyone.

An alarm suddenly sounded, making all three of them nearly jump out of their skins.

Jon drew to a stop and pulled out his phone. 'The first blast,' he said gravely. 'Six seconds ... *Five* ... *Four* ... *Three* ... *Two* ... '

In the distance, a shrill flock of birds erupted from the trees.

Aidan felt the tiniest tremor, like a slight vibration in the air. Almost as soon as it had come, it was gone.

None of them moved. Just stood in a stunned silence.

It had happened, thought Aidan.

Despite all the months of petitions and the protests.

They hadn't been able to stop the fracking.

Aidan thought about Mr Williams; all the people who'd tried. The campaigns and the canvassing.

It had all been for nothing.

Aidan's fists clenched. They might not have stopped this first fracking, he told himself, and he was probably going to have to move away from Carrus – he knew that now – but they could stop any more plans Enershale had. If they could only find Boudicca's tomb, they could expose Berryman for what he was; get proof that the daughters' bones and bracelet had been stolen. Get justice for Robbie. That was what was important now.

Emmi pointed through a gap in the branches. The tall, thin gas stack of the Enershale plant was in view, and from the top of the chimney Aidan saw a blue flame burning against the cloudy sky.

'The first extracted gas,' muttered Jon, with more than a tinge of wonder. 'The methane being burnt.'

'Fifteen minutes until the second blast.' Aidan said. 'Let's go!'

Centurion seemed to sense the urgency, Aidan and his friends jogging as the animal broke into a surprisingly brisk walk.

But at the border of the clearing, Aidan felt Centurion tug back on the rope and refuse to enter. No amount of pulling could persuade him to step over the boundary of bracken and heather. He stamped his front hooves snorting, and would not go any further.

'What is it, boy?' Aidan's heart thudded. 'We've not got time for this!'

He exchanged worried glances with Emmi and Jon, but nobody wanted to offer an explanation. They were all nervous enough as it was.

Aidan tied Centurion to a tree in a sheltered area. He held the horse's head between his hands. 'Wait here. Stay quiet!'

Aidan crouched at the entrance to the tomb chamber, then looked round at Emmi and Jon.

'Go for it, Aide, man,' said Jon in barely a whisper,

patting him on the back. Emmi passed the torch.

With a deep breath, Aidan eased himself between the ancient tree roots and down the stairwell, his two friends following close behind.

The torch cast an eerie glow along the passage walls, and their shadows rose and fell like dark ghosts around them. At one point Aidan thought he heard noises coming from the way they'd come – the sound of footfalls – and he swung the torch beam back fast, only to see Emmi and Jon's startled faces and the black hole of the tunnel stretching behind them.

'You nearly gave me a heart attack, Aide!' said Jon, shielding his eyes with his hand. Then he twisted and let out a scream. 'Spider! Get it off me! Get it off!'

But it was only a clump of roots that had dropped on him from the ceiling.

They picked up their pace, in places Aidan stumbling over lumps of earth that must have come loose since they were last there. He couldn't help shining the torch upwards as they went, seeing the cracks, which seemed to have lengthened and widened.

They entered the chamber, and Aidan hurriedly emptied the tools out of the bag. He took the mallet. 'Let's spread out! Take a section of the far wall each, like Emmi said.

Start low, near the floor and work your way up!'

He banged at the stone and earth, trying to detect a change in sound, Emmi snatched up the claw hammer, and Jon the crowbar, and the two of them did the same either side of him.

But their wall tapping was coming up with nothing.

An alarm reverberated round the chamber.

Jon snatched out his phone. 'Fracking blast number two coming up!' His voice rose as he spoke.

'*Six ... five ... four ... three ...*'

All three of them froze. Aidan's jaw clenched.

'*Two ... one ...*'

There was no mistaking the tremor this time. The air in the confined space wobbled. A tremble rippled up through the soles of Aidan's shoes.

He thought about that thick red line on Berryman's map. Each deep blast getting nearer to where they were. Closing in on them. And if they had felt something that evident with only blast number two, what was going to happen when blast six, that last one, hit?

'Let's keep searching,' said Emmi with a strained voice. 'Hurry!'

The three bent to their work. The air was heavy with tension as they scoured at the chamber walls.

Jon's phone gave its next shrill warning, and Aidan winced with actual physical pain.

'That's fifteen minutes gone already?' protested Emmi. 'It can't be!'

'Blast three,' Jon muttered. *'Five ... four ... three ...'*

Aidan braced. He saw Emmi clutch her hammer tight.

'Two ... one ...'

The chamber shook below them, the vibration rippling up the walls and over their heads. A clod of soil fell from the ceiling and shattered into pieces. A crack snaked up the wall. Aidan heard the unnerving sounds of rock grating rock; stones loosening.

Jon gave a kind of squeak.

Enough messing about! Aidan gritted his teeth and swung the mallet hard. A patch of rock shattered.

He drew back the mallet to swing again ...

They had to find a way through this wall ... before the blasts did it for them and buried them right underneath it.

Jon said he got the [illegible] [illegible] and Aidan [illegible] [illegible] [illegible] paid.

That [illegible] moments gone already [illegible] [illegible] [illegible]

[illegible] [illegible] [illegible]

[illegible] the new [illegible] [illegible] [illegible] [illegible]

[illegible]

The [illegible] [illegible] below [illegible] the [illegible] [illegible] up in the [illegible] [illegible] over their heads. A clod of soil fell from the ceiling and shattered into pieces. A crack [illegible] the walls. Aidan heard the [illegible] [illegible] [illegible] ascending.

[illegible] [illegible]

[illegible] alone! Aidan [illegible] his teeth [illegible] his hand. A [illegible] of rock [illegible].

[illegible] the [illegible] [illegible] [illegible].

They had to find a way through this wall. [illegible] [illegible] [illegible] [illegible] [illegible] [illegible]

23

INTRUDERS

ZERO

There was the dull boom, like a distant explosion, and the muffled vibration of it reverberating through the rocks around them. The throb of it set Aidan's teeth on edge. The space shuddered, and he heard the hollow growling echo of the blast.

Blast four.

Crumbled earth showered down on them, and they had to dodge finger-sized flakes of falling rock.

The grim reality of the situation hit him.

'You have to get out!' he told Emmi and Jon. 'It's getting too dangerous!' He tapped about on a patch of wall they hadn't tried yet, then slammed the section of wall with his mallet – once, twice. 'I'll stay here and keep looking a bit and – '

'No way!' chorused his friends.

'Are you *crazy*?' cried Emmi. 'We're not leaving you here

by yourself, Aidan!'

'I think we should *all* evacuate!' said Jon. His hair stuck up in wild tufts flecked with soil. 'We tried our best. But even if there *is* a weak point through to Boudicca's chamber, we're stuffed. We'll never find it and break through in time.'

Aidan gripped the handle of the mallet then let it go loose in his hand. He hung his head.

This had been their last chance. Their very last chance to find the truth.

Reluctantly, he nodded.

His friends weren't going to leave him here. And he couldn't let them risk staying.

Every second they were in here, was a second less of escape time.

Now that Aidan was no longer focused on the search, the space they were in suddenly seemed much smaller than it had before. Claustrophobic. It was as if the walls had inched forward when he wasn't looking, little by little, squeezing the air. The need to get out gripped him. 'Come on!'

But as Aidan made to leave, he drew to a sudden stop, making Jon and Emmi bunch into a huddle behind him.

There was someone in the doorway.

Catching them in the dazzle of their head torch.

Blocking the way.

Aidan put up a hand to shield his eyes, trying to make out who it was. His mind whirred with confusion and fright as he squinted at the shadowy figure. Had Berryman somehow followed them?

No, that outline wasn't Berryman's.

Was it the accomplice then – some Enershale person?

'Hello kids,' came a voice.

A woman's voice.

'Thank goodness I found you!'

24

HOPE TO DIE

Aidan gaped.

It was Emmi's incredulous voice that spoke first.

'*Miss Carter?*'

The teacher angled her head torch so that the beam wasn't right in their faces. She was still dressed as Boudicca. 'I'm so glad that you're all OK.'

'How did you know we were here, Miss?' said Emmi.

Miss Carter looked at them, a confused look creasing her pretty face. Locks of wavy red hair fell across it. 'Don't you remember?'

Emmi was staring hard at the woman. She repeated her question, more loudly. 'How did you know we were here?'

Aidan saw Jon take an ever-so-slight step backwards.

'You told me,' Miss Carter replied, 'when you came round to my house, Emmi, sweetheart! You told me about finding this old cave, and that you were dead keen to explore it. I told you not to, but I knew you wouldn't listen.

You're just like me – you love adventures too much!'

'Cave?' repeated Jon, looking at Aidan and Emmi.

Aidan's throat went tight. *What was Miss Carter talking about?* He eyed the cracks; then their only exit behind Miss Carter.

'Er ... ' Jon coughed, a dry-sounding cough. He was blinking hard and Aidan noticed that one of his legs had started trembling. 'We need to leave now, Miss Carter. We can talk more about this when we get out where it's safe.' He took a shaky step towards her.

'Stay where you are, Jon.'

The teacher had lifted something to waist level, and at first Aidan couldn't believe what he was seeing. But it was caught in the torchlight so there couldn't be any mistaking it.

Miss Carter was holding a gun.

And she was pointing it right in their direction.

Aidan stared as the realisation sunk in.

Emmi's face wore a look of disgust. 'Robbie's accident,' she said, her voice acid. 'Did you by any chance have something to do with that?'

'Ah, Emmi,' Miss Carter sighed. 'Sweetheart,' she said, in that same sing-song voice.

Aidan's mind went into overdrive. He thought about making a grab for the gun, but he couldn't risk it going off with all of them in such a confined space ... There wasn't enough room to get round Miss Carter ...

'We deserve an explanation at least!' demanded Emmi. Her shock echoed through the chamber. Angry tears streamed down her face. 'After what happened to my cousin, I deserve to know the truth!'

There was a pause. Miss Carter sighed again. Then Aidan saw her expression harden. There was an ugly twist to her mouth as she spoke.

'Robbie and I found this site. When we were children.

'It wasn't long after he got that virus that damaged his brain. He followed me around everywhere I went, like a little dog. Poor, stupid Robbie.'

Aidan saw Emmi's hands clench into fists by her sides, but she stayed silent.

'We saw the steps,' Miss Carter went on, 'but could only guess at what was beyond them. It was impossible to get through – believe me, we tried! We made it a game to guess what was down here.

'But I couldn't get rid of Robbie. It got quite tedious. So sometimes I would trap him down between the roots and tell him they were snakes going to get him.' She gave a mechanical little laugh. 'He used to get so scared, silly Robbie, and it was only a game! He should have known it was just a game, shouldn't he?'

She shifted her position and the gun twitched.

'But one night there was a huge storm and a landslide in the clearing, and the whole entrance was covered up so you couldn't see the steps any more.

'And Robbie and I swore to each other, cross our hearts and hope to die, to keep the place a secret. Our special secret.'

Her eyes glinted in the torchlight.

'*Cross our hearts, and hope to die,*' she repeated, in a cold monotone.

Aidan's skin crawled.

'But why didn't you tell anyone?' he said stiffly. 'Even when you grew up? You must have guessed what this place could be.'

Miss Carter regarded him a minute.

'Don't you like having secrets?' she asked. 'Old Centurion and his poor injured leg, for example?' Aidan flinched. 'Doesn't *everyone* like having precious secrets?'

She scowled suddenly. 'But then Robbie must have somehow got down here without asking my permission. Dug and wriggled his way through like the little weasel he is; I don't know how he did it. He took the arm bracelet and put it in the museum without telling me.' Aidan heard her voice spiked with anger. 'It wasn't his place to decide.'

'I had to take the bracelet before someone found out its significance. I had to stop him blabbing to everyone. I didn't have a choice.'

'We always have choices,' Emmi said.

'Do you know about ghosts, children?' Miss Carter said. '*You* do, Aidan.' She turned to him. 'Losing your mum the way you did.'

'Don't you talk about my mum!'

'Ruins a childhood, a thing like that,' Miss Carter continued. 'Childhood ghosts are the worst kind there are. But believe me, if you'd had parents like mine, you would have wanted to leave home and get right away from this place. I was glad when they died.'

Aidan shuddered. The most shocking part wasn't what she was saying, it was the way she was saying it. So matter-of-fact; without any emotion.

'All I wanted was to leave Carrus. But then I found out about all the debts my so loving parents had left me saddled with.'

'Who knocked down Robbie?' interruped Aidan, feeling braver than he sounded. 'Was it you or Berryman?'

Miss Carter gave that tinkling laugh again. 'Berryman? That conceited loser!'

Emmi shot Aidan a confused look. 'Or some Enershale traitor, then?' she stammered.

'I assure you,' said Miss Carter. 'I prefer to work alone. Why would I want to share the money with anyone, if I didn't have to?'

'But ... ' Aidan just didn't get it. *She had to be wrong, didn't she?* 'But, it was *Berryman* who was going to make loads of money from the Enershale deals.'

'Was it?' said Miss Carter mildly.

'We saw the contract at the manor house!' snapped Emmi.

Aidan put a hand on Emmi's arm. He thought back to the document they'd found in the Lord's study. What had it said again? Emmi's voice spooled through his mind: ' ... *four million pounds ... paid to the landowner of adjacent land ... Berryman agrees to cooperate fully with any expansion of operations* – '

His mouth went dry. It hadn't *actually* said that the landowner of adjacent land was Berryman himself, had it?

Berryman had agreed to *cooperate*, but that wasn't the same thing.

'A manager from Enershale came to my door,' Miss Carter continued. 'He knew fracking would be controversial in the community, so he was only too happy to keep the deal confidential.'

'So the concerned school teacher and anti-fracking protests were all just a big act,' Emmi said bitterly.

Aidan stood there, stunned. Everything suddenly made appalling sense. Miss Carter's cottage was right next to the fracking zone. It was such a small house that he'd never have imagined all that surrounding land also belonged to her.

The *landowner of the adjacent land*, the person set to gain huge sums from Enershale's expansion plans ... it wasn't Berryman.

It was Alice Carter!

Miss Carter gave him a pitying look.

'I'm sorry about the black eye, Aidan,' she said. 'If only you hadn't come back home when you did. But I couldn't let you work out it was my car on the lane that day.'

'*You?*' Emmi could hardly get the word out.

Miss Carter ignored her. 'I like you kids,' she said. 'You're clever. You deserved to know the truth before ... ' Her voice trailed off.

'Before what?' said Aidan. But she didn't answer.

He swallowed. All he could think of was what Miss Carter had done to Robbie; the gun in her hand; the robotic look in the woman's eyes ...

'You still haven't told us how you knew we were here,'

he said, trying to buy time.

'I needed to know what you were up to,' she answered. 'Keep track of where you were going.' A small smile played on her lips. 'Can't you guess how?'

Emmi gasped suddenly, rifling through her pocket. She brought out the carved hare Miss Carter had given her at the cottage, and with a cry threw it down on the ground.

It fell with such force that the wood split open.

Jon bent to pick something up that had shot from the broken carving. He examined the small object then held it up between shaky fingers. 'GPS device,' he said in a small voice.

Aidan stared at the smashed hare. She'd been tracking them all along!

'And it was me, wasn't it, who told you about the drone,' added Jon sheepishly, 'while we were at your house?'

'Don't blame yourself, Jon,' Miss Carter soothed. 'But it was pointless for you to come down here, children. I removed all the bones and relocated them, along with the bracelet.'

Aidan swapped quick glances with Emmi and Jon. *She doesn't know!*

Miss Carter didn't know about the clue in the riddle. About Boudicca's tomb being next to this one. *Course she doesn't know! How could she?*

'The new Iceni-Roman battle site has been established,' Miss Carter continued. She shifted the gun a little, flicking a strand of red hair from her eyes with her free hand. 'You've done nothing but put yourselves in awful danger, children.'

Emmi's eyes were fixed on the barrel. 'If you kill us, they'll find out you did it,' she spat.

Miss Carter drew away from them with a look of dismay, the gun lowered again. She put a hand to her mouth and shook her head. 'I'm not going to *kill* you. What are you *thinking*? Why would you say that; I could never do that!'

Aidan's spine prickled as she spoke. There was something so unnatural about it, as if she was reciting words she'd rehearsed for one of her plays.

'We all have to get out,' Miss Carter said urgently, looking around wildly as if this idea had only just occurred to her. 'As soon as we can.'

Aidan realised what the woman was doing: convincing herself that this tomb would be to blame for what happened to them; nothing to do with her.

'I came looking for you,' Miss Carter repeated, backing towards the tomb exit. 'I tried to help you, but Jon hurt himself, and then the shockwave from the fracking blast came and … I tried to help you, I really did!'

He imagined the woman clutching a hot cup of tea and sobbing convincingly as she had to recount the story to the emergency services. Would that be the tale she told the police, Aidan wondered, as a team tried to dig out their dead bodies?

More likely, she'd just say nothing. Three missing kids, disappeared without a trace.

Jon's warning alarm blared. *Blast five.*

'The hospital have told me I can visit Robbie,' Miss Carter said quietly, and there was something about the way she said it that made Aidan feel sick.

'You stay away from my cousin!' shouted Emmi furiously. 'If you do anything to Robbie again, I'll … ' She took a step towards Miss Carter and Aidan saw the woman's hand grip the gun.

'*Seven … six … five …* ' recited Jon under his breath in a panic.

'Robbie didn't suffer,' Miss Carter soothed. 'He was knocked out, darling, as soon as he hit my windscreen.'

Emmi threw herself at Miss Carter with a cry. There was a blur of movement. Aidan was momentarily too stunned to react.

The gun went off with a deafening crack. Something

glanced Aidan's arm, stinging the skin. He heard Jon cry out. Emmi screamed. He saw Miss Carter escaping down the passageway ...

And a fraction of a second later ...

... the blast hit.

25

TRAPPED

The shockwave rippled up through the depths. Aidan's teeth rattled. Emmi was clutching his arm so tight it hurt.

There was a wrenching crack. A scream he couldn't place. Aidan crouched; his hands curled instinctively up round his head. He heard Jon give a small, scared cry. Stones pelted from overhead. A rock glanced his side.

Slowly, after what felt like forever, the trembling subsided.

Aidan coughed. There was the taste of grit in his mouth. He blinked; the feeble beam of his torch picking out the swirling motes of dust in the chamber. Soil showered down in a thin stream like sand from an hourglass.

There was a sharp pain in his arm when he moved it, and he saw a sliver of stone jutting from his sleeve, embedded in his skin. A bit of rock shattered by the ricocheting bullet, he guessed. Flinching, he eased it out.

Aidan heard a weak voice, Jon's: 'Man down.' And he went over to where his friend was lying.

'Jon!' Emmi cried, rushing to his side.

'It's just a graze,' gasped Jon, clutching his ankle, his face screwed up. 'Flesh wound.'

Aidan exchanged anxious glances with Emmi. There was a tear at the bottom of Jon's jeans, and blood round the hole where Miss Carter's bullet had hit.

Emmi's eyes were round with shock. She took off her hoodie and got busy wrapping the fabric round the wound.

Aidan helped her wind the material tight, then stared round the chamber.

The plinth of the doorway had collapsed, strewing the gap with a barrier of rubble and earth, blocking their escape.

But it was the buckled ceiling that worried him most. Stone slabs were wedged precariously against each other like tumbled, giant grey dominoes.

He saw Jon shiver as Emmi finished tying his makeshift, bulky bandage. 'My ankle hurts.'

'Stay still, Jon,' said Aidan quickly, putting the holdall under his head as a pillow.

'Miss Carter got away!' said Emmi, twisting her hands together. 'She said she was going to see Robbie. I've got to warn Mum and Dad! Tell the police!'

She tugged out her mobile, but Aidan held her arm. 'There's no signal down here, Em,' he said gently. 'Remember?'

Emmi clambered towards the entranceway, waggling at pieces of stone and earth that blocked it.

Aidan joined in, lifting chunks out and lugging them to one side.

They heaved and scraped at the rubble.

'Sorry I can't help, guys,' Jon croaked. His face was pale. He winced as he eased his mobile out of his pocket and checked the timer.

'One blast left,' he mumbled, his eyes huge and staring at the ceiling. 'Thirteen minutes and thirteen seconds.'

Aidan worked faster. He fumbled with a loose rock, a fingernail tearing painfully against the abrasive surface. The cloying taste of damp earth coated the back of his throat.

He clamped his hands round a jutting stone and, gritting his teeth, eased it towards him. As he pulled it free it triggered a small landslide and he and Emmi drew back quickly, watching the flurry tensely, waiting for it to settle. They stood there in an uneasy silence.

Experimentally, Aidan reached a hand into one of the fist-sized spaces.

Another small landslide made them freeze.

Aidan stumbled back and shook his head. 'We have to stop. The whole lot could go. There's no getting out that way.'

He and Emmi sat on the ground, panting. Aidan struggled to control the fear rising through his chest; the crawling claustrophobia in the dying torch light.

Shadows seemed to circle him, their darkness deepening the fissures; the spider-thread crack right up the far wall.

Gnawing rat voices scurried through his head. *You're trapped. There's no way out. You're all going to die down here.*

He chewed the inside of his cheek and tried to focus on a plan, any plan.

But none came.

Emmi was standing in the middle of the chamber, a dazed expression on her face.

Aidan saw her run her fingers over the inscription in the rock Robbie had made.

BP.

The next second she had snatched up a pointed stone and was bent to the rock surface, scratching energetically.

'Em,' said Aidan, 'what are you doing?'

'If we don't get out of here ... ' Emmi sniffed and pushed the hair from her face. Her voice was thick. 'If they dig us out and find this place, I want them to know the truth – my mum and dad – about everything that's happened.' Her voice wobbled. 'So one day, somehow, they'll know the truth about us and Robbie and everything, and Miss Carter won't get away with what she's done.'

She continued to scrape unhappily at the surface, grazing her knuckles with the effort. She gave a small sob, and began to hack at the stone more aggressively, driving the rock point forward, stabbing letters one by one into the wall.

ALICE CARTER MURD ...

Aidan watched her, a chaotic mix of emotions shunting painfully through him.

He saw Jon silently staring at Emmi too, his eyes glistening.

Aidan thought about his dad; losing Mum had nearly killed him, and now ...

Aidan thought about his two friends who'd stuck by him, no matter what.

I'll get them out, he told himself fiercely. *I'll get Emmi and Jon out.*

Jon gave a yelp as Aidan grabbed his top and slid him along the floor, away from the worst of the warped ceiling and into a small alcove at the chamber edge, where a lip of harder rock might give some protection.

Emmi finished her message, and she and Aidan huddled over Jon, shielding him.

I'll get them out ... Aidan repeated the words like a mantra. But each time he said them, his voice came out a little weaker, as if the hope was draining out of him.

He was to blame for Jon and Emmi being here. It was he – Aidan – that Boudicca and her daughters had sought out. Had this been their plan all along? To lure him here, get them all killed? Some kind of warped human sacrifice for a reason he couldn't even begin to guess at.

Aidan was filled with crushing doubt. Boudicca had probably murdered her share of people when she was alive, after all. Defending her land, maybe, but she had been a killer just the same.

And if the ghosts weren't against them, where were they now, when he most needed them?

'*Valour! Truth!*'

Aidan called the words out loud and heard them echo round the purple darkness of the chamber.

The three of them gripped each other.

The torch sent out a dim blueish beam that settled in a thin pool against the far wall, catching the message Emmi had scraped on to the stone.

ALICE CARTER MURDERED US

HER CAR HIT ROBBIE PICKERSGILL

FOUR MILLION FRACKING MONEY

Her work had widened the crack running up the rock. Now it was the width of a fist.

Aidan stared. Blinked. He must be hallucinating. There was light showing through the long crack. A light that couldn't be from the torch. Shakily, he got to his feet.

He moved nearer. But he still couldn't work out what it was.

'Aidan?' Emmi whispered.

The light was coming from the other side. Sunlight? But how could it be? Some kind of light, reflected at strange angles.

Aidan put his hands to the wall and pressed his eye to the gap ...

'How much time do we have left?' He could hardly speak the words. His heart thumped against the rock surface.

'Nine, ten minutes,' wheezed Jon. 'But ... '

Aidan grabbed the claw hammer, and swung it hard at the fissure, one smack followed immediately by another.

'What are you *doing*, Aidan!' Emmi cried in alarm. 'What is it? It's not safe to ... '

The edges of the crack began to fall away like flaking plaster. Slate-like strata fragmented under the blows, as one edge was cleaved off, the next coming away ... until the gap was wide enough; just wide enough to squeeze through.

Aidan looked at his friends. Emmi's mouth was gaping. Jon had lifted his head slightly. None of them said a word. They didn't need to.

Aidan and Emmi quickly helped Jon up. His bandaged foot scraped the ground as he limped to the opening, an arm round each of their shoulders.

Then one by one, with much twisting and pushing and gasps of pain, the three of them went through into the chamber beyond.

26

LAY HER TO REST

The first thing Aidan made out was the curving metal of some kind of wheel. The rim of a chariot wheel, he realised, its wood long since perished.

Sunlight came from the ceiling, an opening several metres up, from which thick roots dangled. Through the hole Aidan saw the branches of the horse chestnut tree; a ragged leaf canopy and patches of sky. A hole that must have opened up in the tremor. A weak patch of ground collapsed.

As Aidan's eyes adjusted, other objects materialised from the gloom, reflecting the light.

The three stood speechless.

Shields, intricately carved with swirling, interlocking Celtic patterns.

Ornate, tarnished spear tips. Drinking cups studded with gems. Jewellery stacked in piles.

Everywhere, there was the shimmer of silver, of gold.

And in the chamber's centre ...

'Target located,' Jon croaked. 'Operation Tomb Boudicca is ... ' Aidan felt Jon's legs buckle, and he and Emmi set him on the ground, gazing.

Aidan's throat tightened.

Undisturbed for 2,000 ...

The three shuffled closer ...

A raised stone slab.

A human skeleton, laid out in funeral pose.

Aidan saw the skull, with a gold band set round it; the bones of a ribcage, leg bones, arm bones. The skeleton fingers of one hand grasping something.

'Oh my god,' Emmi breathed.

Aidan stared too, the metal blade; the swirling hare engraved on its hilt. A sword. A huge red gem glimmering from the hare's eye.

Boudicca's sword.

Aidan snapped his mind back to what had to be done.

'We can get out!' He tugged hard at one of the dangling roots. It might just take his weight. He pushed the strand into Jon's hands and wrapped his friend's fingers hurriedly round it. 'Get a grip of this root, Jon-Boy. Go on!'

Jon clutched the root, and gave a grunt as he tried to climb. Aidan made a stirrup with his hand and launched him by his good foot, and Jon squirmed in the air trying in vain to get a grip on the pitted stone walls.

'Try again, Jon!' Emmi insisted, trying to lift him.

'Can't!' Jon said, flopping to the ground. 'No good.'

'You go up first, Aidan,' Emmi said. 'Then you can help to pull him up!'

Aidan looked at her a moment, then he grabbed the tree root and was clinging to it, heaving himself upwards, using the hand stirrup Emmi made for him to gain height. Then his feet were on her shoulders and he felt Emmi wobble under him, and he was grappling and pulling himself, grunting with the effort, getting another, then another, foothold in the pitted stone wall of the chamber, reaching for the space and clawing his way out ... Squeezing, pushing out through the frame of coiling bracken and heather.

He came out on his back, and lay there a short moment, getting his breath back, the ancient branches of the horse chestnut tree arching over him.

Then he rushed to pull out his phone.

Still no signal. How could that be?

Aidan pulled himself on to his front and leant into the hole, stretching down with an arm. 'Come on, Jon!'

Jon cried out as he tried again to climb. His face was

ash grey. He shook his head, crumpling. 'I'll never get up there. You go, Em,' he panted. 'I'll wait here.'

'Jon, there's no way am I leaving you here alone. Aidan!' she said in a rush. 'Get to the fracking platform. Tell them about the tomb; about us being trapped here.'

Jon clutched his mobile phone, as if willing the countdown to stop. The light from the screen illuminated his sweaty forehead. 'Yeah, Aide,' he mumbled. 'You can do it.'

Aidan's mind spun.

'Take proof!' Emmi called up. Her face was fierce with determination.

He saw her reach over the body. Light glanced off the sword as she lifted it, then hurriedly strapped it to the end of a hanging root.

Aidan hoisted up the blade.

He untied the sword and slotted it into the belt of his jeans; the weight of it giving him a strange courage. 'How long do we have?' He fumbled for his watch to set the timer.

'Five minutes,' Jon called falteringly.

'You can do this, Aidan!' Emmi shouted.

But they all knew the truth.

Even at full sprint, it would take a miracle for Aidan to get to the Enershale platform in time.

Aidan crouched by the hole. 'I'm coming back,' he shouted to them. 'His voice echoed round the chamber. I'm coming back for you!'

Emmi nodded hard, tears in her eyes as she looked up at him. 'Course!' Her voice broke with emotion. 'Course you are, Aide!'

There was a sound from above Aidan as he stood to go. A snort.

Centurion!

Somehow he'd got loose from where he'd been tethered; the rope dangling from the horse's bridle; his head tossing so that his mane moved in tangles.

A wild hope stirred through Aidan.

In his mind he saw Robbie's face with its mischievous smile. '*Miracles happen.*'

But the leg – it still wasn't properly healed. What if they fell again? What if ...

Centurion nuzzled Aidan with force, nearly knocking him backwards.

Aidan thought of Jon lying injured. Emmi bravely waiting with him; the final blast ...

He gave Centurion a heavy pat then swung himself up on to the horse's back.

He felt the animal stagger a little under his weight,

Aidan swaying clumsily as he struggled to get his balance with the sword. Then Centurion stood steady, straightening without complaint; ears pointed and alert.

Aidan gripped the mane as the horse gave a few lurching steps.

His eyes flicked to his watch. *Four minutes twenty-nine seconds ...*

'I'm riding Centurion!' he shouted in the direction of the hole. 'I'll get there in time!' He tried to make his promise sound sure, muffling his thick panic.

And the two of them set off at a skittish trot, out of the clearing and into the dense hem of trees.

A hoof caught on a stone, making Centurion stumble. But the horse righted himself and continued on, picking up speed as they weaved between the trees.

27

INTO BATTLE

Three minutes ... Aidan felt Centurion build speed towards a gallop.

At every twist and turn of the path, Aidan tensed and held his breath, the horse's leg jarring slightly on the swerving corners.

But now that Centurion was in motion, the horse seemed to be relishing the run, sensing the urgency, finding his rhythm – instinct taking over.

All the same, Aidan pressed himself tight against the animal's back.

Jon. Emmi.

Branches whipped his face. Leaves blocked his view. The sword swung awkwardly at his hip, threatening to destabilise him.

Aidan gripped with his knees, and urged the animal on with a shout. He felt a rumble, deep in Centurion's throat, and they picked up more speed, the horse taking lunging strides, sods of moss torn up by his hooves as he went.

They broke out from the woods and veered along the steel mesh of the perimeter fence. The sign, *RESTRICTED AREA*, flashed past. There was the blur of the Enershale eagle on its flagpole, wings outstretched. The drilling tower loomed up; the tall chimney with its ghostly blue flare. The raised drilling platform with its box-like cabins.

Two minutes ...

They reached the entrance and Centurion drew to a snorting halt at the neck-high gate, barbed wire coiled along its top.

Ninety seconds ...

'Stop the fracking!' Aidan yelled as a security guard ambled out from the hut.

The man regarded him in surprise, then folded his arms across his chest. 'Don't think so, sonny. My orders are to let nobody through. Especially not today.'

'My friends are trapped!' Aidan cried. 'You have to let me in! Open the gate!'

But the man just stared at him blankly.

'We found Queen Boudicca's tomb!' cried Aidan, desperate to make the man understand. 'It's about to collapse with my friends inside!'

The guard raised his eyebrows. Rolled his eyes.

'I have her sword!' Aidan struggled to take it from the belt of his jeans to show him, but the guard had already turned away, was speaking into his walkie-talkie; asking to be put through to the police ...

One minute ...

Aidan needed to get to the platform, to the control room. Talk to the people who really mattered. He urged Centurion away from the gate, appearing to be leaving.

But when they were a few dozen metres away, he turned the two of them sharply to again face the entrance.

He kicked the horse's sides with a cry.

Centurion broke into a run. They careered forward, Aidan bracing himself low as the wind rushed past the sides of his head and the horse's mane streamed into his face.

Forty-five seconds ...

His pulse raced.

Come on!

Aidan heard Centurion's rasping breaths; felt the frenzy of hooves under him.

The gate loomed up but there was no stopping now.

He grasped Centurion's neck and braced.

He felt the horse's body lift; the heavy weightlessness as they left the ground.

Time seemed to slow down, stretching into slow motion the terror of the jump.

Then the prickle of elation as he realised ...

They'd cleared the gate!

Centurion slammed down the other side of the barrier. Aidan was thrown forward. He tucked and rolled, hitting the ground hard, right on his arm.

There was the sound of snapping bone, a shock of agony.

He saw the sword flung away from him, sliding across the gravel surface of the compound; Centurion stamping and tossing his head.

Aidan struggled up to a sitting position. 'Stop!' His left arm hung at a strange angle at the elbow. It dangled uselessly by his side as he pulled himself to his feet and staggered towards the largest of the work cabins. He made for its metal steps, for the sword that had come to rest at the bottom.

Thirty seconds ...

'Stop the fracking!' he yelled.

He was almost passing out from the pain, but he forced himself on. His friends' faces loomed in his mind. *Jon. Emmi. Jon. Emmi.* His promise to get them out.

He reached the sword but it was suddenly so heavy, he could hardly lift it. Instead he dragged it by the hilt.

A face appeared at a window of the cabin, then another.

The door at the top of the steps flew open. A man in a hard hat stood there, staring down at him.

'Stop!' Aidan yelled. He felt a terrible panic that they'd make no sense of his tumbling words ... 'We found Queen Boudicca's tomb ... in a clearing in Carrus Woods ... going to collapse ... my friends are trapped ... right above the last blast ... '

The man's face clouded, unreadable. The other faces at the windows continued to stare.

Fifteen seconds ...

With a last, desperate effort, Aidan lifted the sword.

With a grunt he heaved it upright.

Held its point straight.

Higher.

Higher still.

Where the light came from, afterwards no one could exactly say.

Some said it was a rogue beam of sunlight; others, a reflection from a site flood lamp.

But in that strange instant, light hit the sword and the ancient blade glowed.

The leaping hare along its hilt stood out in startling definition. The blood-like dazzle of the ruby sparked like fire.

An energy rippled along Aidan's raised arm, a stinging intensity, but still he gripped the sword.

He saw the stunned face of the man at the door. Heard him shout something to a colleague and sprint back inside.

Aidan crumpled to his knees, and the sword fell.

'You have to stop the last blast!' It came out in almost a whisper now. Black dots fizzled across his vision.

He saw the gas flare, soaring blue flame blurring as it speared the sky; saw three birds skim across it.

And then he couldn't make it out any more; couldn't make out anything.

Time seemed to merge; the past and present became one dark swirl.

He was being lifted, carried ...

Laid to rest.

And later – how much later, he could not tell – as he shifted in and out of shadows, he heard snatches of voices. Shocked words.

'Emergency services rushed to the clearing.'

'They've pulled someone out ...

'But they died on the way to hospital.'

28

WARRIORS

Aidan looked out from his vantage point on the small hill, over the lush-looking fields towards Carrus Woods. The morning light illuminated the treetops, highlighting the vivid green mosaic of its canopy.

He flexed the fingers of his left hand. The arm still felt tender from the hospital removing the plaster, but his break had healed OK.

Jon rolled over on to his back, a blade of grass in the corner of his mouth. 'It was great news about Robbie. You got to see him this morning, right Emmi?'

She clasped her hands together. 'He opened his eyes and the first thing he said ... ' she giggled a bit. 'He asked where his shrew's skull was!'

Aidan gave a laugh. 'He's definitely getting better then!'

He watched a bird fly across the patch of sky where the Enershale gas flare chimney used to be. The whole site had been dismantled, and all that was left were shapes on the ground like some kind of archaeological site; a square where the drilling platform had been, and a few smaller rectangles marking out the removed work cabins.

In a few months, Aidan mused, it would all be overgrown. In a few years, it would be as if the entire plant had never existed at all.

There was the distant sound of an engine, and he watched a van pulling up by scaffolding; the moving specks of people already at work.

'It's going to be amazing,' said Emmi. 'The new museum they're building in place of the old one. I can't wait for it to be finished!'

'Yeah,' said Jon. 'Mr Williams was practically crying tears of joy when they showed him the plans.'

'And what about Lord Berryman?' Emmi rolled her eyes. 'What a turnaround *that* was!'

'Fracking Warrior to Proud Historian in a matter of minutes!' Jon sniggered. 'Once Berryman realised the money he can make from tourism, there was no contest!'

Aidan smiled. He looked towards Berryman's mansion, surrounded by its gardens, the horse paddock, the meadow, the stables.

His and Dad's house in the grounds.

His and Dad's house.

'You should have heard Berryman boasting to a news team in the village!' said Emmi. 'Telling them how it's his land at the very centre of Boudicca's last great battle, now a major World Heritage Site. From the way he was talking, you'd think it was him who single-handedly found her tomb!'

'You'll never guess what his new idea is,' smirked Aidan. 'Horse-drawn chariot rides!'

All three of them erupted into laughing fits.

'No joke!' said Aidan. 'He's already bought six new horses. He practically begged Dad to stay on and manage the stables.'

'I was never really going to get rid of Centurion you know, Aidan!' recited Jon, doing a perfect impression of Lord Berryman's slightly whiney voice. 'You got the wrong end of the stick *completely*!'

Emmi wagged a finger with a frown, continuing the impersonation. 'I was of course not happy about being left in the dark, I grant you, Aidan, but when I phoned the vet, it was simply to come and check the horse's condition and decide on further treatment.'

Aidan smiled. He remembered those other things James Berryman had said as well; later, when it had just been the two of them. '*Struck a chord with me, Aidan, I have to tell you; the way you talked about Centurion being your mum's favourite horse ... and it was a brave thing you did for your friends. Very brave ... And as a gesture, to show there're no hard feelings between us, I'd like to give you and your dad a gift ...'*

Aidan shielded the sun from his eyes and squinted at the shapes down below in the distant paddock. The horses grazing there.

The new horses. Firefly, Fenland Queen. Centurion.

Emotion swelled through him.

Centurion is my horse now!

He could still barely believe it.

Emmi lay back on the grass, her arms tucked behind her head. 'How's Centurion's leg now, Aidan?'

'Riding him obviously wasn't the best thing for it,' he said. 'But Ann says he's responding really well to the treatment. She couldn't believe how well.'

'I think I'm going to pull through too,' croaked Jon, gripping his ankle theatrically. 'But only just.'

'Hey, did you see the article in this?' Emmi tapped Jon's head with a rolled-up newspaper. 'I wanted us to look at it together.'

She flattened the paper and read the headline out loud:

FRACKING PLANS ABANDONED AS ANCIENT LAND REVEALS ITS STARTLING SECRETS

After several weeks of careful excavation, the archaeological find described as one of the most significant in Britain, continues to be the centre of intense media attention. The finding of the treasure-laden tomb complex of the legendary Queen Boudicca and her daughters gives answers to a centuries-old mystery about the exact location of her Iceni tribe's uprising against the mighty Roman Empire

But Carrus-under-Hill has not been without its modern-day battles. The village hit headlines during the summer when the government-backed energy company Enershale started fracking operations in the area. But the significance of the find and the overwhelming public interest means that the land has been given immediate protected status.

'Fracking is to stop for the foreseeable future,' the Prime Minister assured the people of Carrus, on a surprise visit to the village yesterday. He however took the opportunity to reiterate the importance of fracking in Britain's energy policy to safeguard the country's future. As heckling from the gathered crowd increased, the PM hastily pledged extra funding for Carrus's new museum, before being taken away by helicopter.

Aidan sniggered. 'The P.M. couldn't leave fast enough, could he?'

The three teenagers, who found the tomb using a remote-controlled drone, have continued to be inundated with requests for interviews.

'Another news team wants to talk to me, by the way.' Jon faked a yawn. 'Oh, just some major international TV channel, you know. Some documentary they want to make about how the tomb was found.' He examined his fingernails, eyebrows raised.

'Me and Dronie in the starring roles, of course.'

He rolled out of range with a yelp as a laughing Emmi swiped at him.

'OK! OK!' he raised his arms in surrender. 'I'll let them interview you too, Em, I promise!'

Aidan gave a sideways grin. 'Not sure we should mention the bit about getting help from a ghost Boudicca and her phantom daughters, though.'

'Uh huh.' Emmi gazed out from the hill. 'They can stay our secret, I think, don't you?'

'All that ghost stuff ... ' began Jon uncertainly. He pulled up a handful of grass as he tried to find the right words. 'It was all so ... well ... '

He gave up trying and flicked the grass at Emmi with a shrug and a smile. 'I guess I have to admit that there are some things that can't be explained by science after all!'

'*It has been revealed,*' said Emmi, continuing with the article, '*that landowner Alice Carter, set to gain substantial sums from Enershale expansion plans, stole the bones of Boudicca's daughters and an arm bracelet in an attempt to lead archaeologists to a false site.*'

Emmi's voice went more serious.

'Carter, who has also now been linked to arson, and a hit-and-run ...'

She bit her lip and passed the paper to Aidan. 'You read the rest,' she said quietly.

Aidan swallowed. '*Carter ... died inside the tomb complex when the section of tunnel she was in collapsed.*'

'I really thought she'd got out,' said Emmi. She pulled at a patch of grass. 'There were rumours that she was horribly injured when they found her, and delirious. She kept saying how two blue flames sprang up inside the passageway and blocked her escape route.'

She gave a stiff little laugh.

'Not that anyone believes that, of course.'

Jon hung his head and said nothing.

'The daughters have now been reunited with their mother.' Aidan read on quietly. '*The three skeletons will be displayed side by side in the new museum.*'

He folded the paper and put it down.

'Do you think they're at peace now?' said Emmi. She looked out towards the woods. 'Boudicca, I mean. And Valour and Truth?'

Aidan followed Emmi's gaze across the fields; the irrigation channels along their edges, mist catching the light like silver stitching. Those tranquil fields where that gory battle had been fought all those centuries ago. The terrible suffering there had been on both sides.

His eyes were drawn to the green, mysterious woods, and the unseen places between the trees.

In a strange way he somehow knew the answer to Emmi's question.

'Yes,' he said. 'Yes, I think they are.'

Aidan watched clouds scud across the sky, then disappear in the bright, morning haze. He breathed deeply, filling his lungs with the smells of the new day. A shaft of sunlight filtered through a gap, casting gold light on to the field that bordered Carrus Woods.

And for a fleeting moment he saw something ...

Aidan sat up straight.

There was a silhouette, of a chariot.

Backlit by the sun's rays. A two-horse chariot, carrying three figures; they looked towards Aidan across the fields, across time ...

He saw the tallest figure – a woman – raise the reins and the horses broke into motion, and Aidan watched, the vision already beginning to vanish.

Reunited with their mother.

The chariot and its riders faded, heading across the fields and towards open fenland. Galloping free.

ACKNOWLEDGEMENTS

Camilla Barnard
Jon Barton
Jane Beagley
John Coefield
Matt Dickinson
Margaret Eastham
Paul Eastham
Anna Elizabeth
Elena Elizabeth
Lorna Hargreaves
Freddie Jobbins
Caroline Johnson
Gill Lewis
Sarah Mussi
Nathan Ryder
Susie Ryder
Caroline Walsh
Steve Wildman

Thank you everyone.
Ethereal beings and treasures all.

Ruth Eastham is an award-winning author from the UK. Her debut novel, *The Memory Cage*, was shortlisted for the Waterstones Children's Book Prize, and won the Inspiration Book Award. Teachers voted it best story in the UK Literacy Association Book Award, and it won and was shortlisted for many other regional prizes. *The Memory Cage* was also nominated for the prestigious Carnegie Medal.

Her second book, *The Messenger Bird,* won and was shortlisted for many local authority book prizes and its Enigma Code themes made it a featured book at the famous Bletchley Park.

Ruth is a popular speaker in schools, in the UK and abroad, fascinating children with the real life mysteries and dramas behind these and her other books: *Arrowhead*, *The Jaguar Trials* and *The Warrior in the Mist.*

Ruth has lived in New Zealand, Australia and Italy and has two daughters. Find out more: **www.rutheastham.com**